The Emperor's Flute

or

The Memoir of Charles Defutois

A Novel of the Eighteenth Century

Thomas Thibeault

Ridgetop Press
55 Diane Lane
Maggie Valley
North Carolina
USA
28751

The Library of Congress has catalogued The Emperor's Flute as follows:

ISBN: 978-0-9836618-2-5

Thibeault, Thomas.
    The Emperor's Flute/Thomas Thibeault

1 Barque Music - fiction.   2. 18th Century - fiction.
3 Frederick the Great - fiction   4. J.J. Quantz - fiction.

When the mode of the music changes,
the walls of the city shake.

Plato

The Memoir of Charles Defutois

Part the First

Paris, Lazarette Prison,

July 24, 1794

He told me that when a man knows he is to be hanged in a fortnight, it concentrates his mind wonderfully. He lied.

When my sentence was pronounced, there was only an explosion. Thoughts became cesspools of regret. Every hope was a trap sprung with despair. I could neither doubt the lies nor believe the truth. My body could not support such terror, and my son later told me that I fell as if dead into his arms. My mind was dead, pressed unto peine forte et dure without hope of relief. A mere breath became a battle and the monster Uncertainty took such malicious joy in my every gasp. I had thought that I would not wish such pain on my worst enemy, but I have since changed my mind.

Throughout this torture, there is Paul, my son. He brings apples to my cell and demands for courage. I tell him, I have little left, and he chuckles with the assurance that he has some to spare. If I chew slowly, the tart loveliness recalls happier times, sweet to the core. I can remember when I had so much more of Paul's gallantry and find some peace. Such a lively child, squirming upon my knee, and I would scour the fruit with a spoon for his insistent lips. Now the child has become the father.

But this accursed place breeds fantastic fears and it is hard to be courageous. Paul is young and thinks we will live forever, and that is a necessary blessing. I am old and know what lies ahead.

I must tell this story to save my sanity. I have no means to record such impressions, for our new masters fear truths foreign to their notions. This new fraternité trembles before words and cowers behind the blade it believes is mightier than the pen. Paper and ink are both suspected of sedition. My tale must hide in memory.

I refuse to leave a record of my times. Let the court chroniclers celebrate the royal blue of His Majesty's eyes, but I saw the joyful malice in those moist orbs. No. I will not rejoice in the triumphs of some crowned rogue. Poetry would help me to make rhymes where there is no reason, but the recitation would be greater than my remaining days. This tale must be preserved in the newest craze, a nouvelle to hold my rage. I can spin this yarn to beat the noose. Surely, the Muses will permit my lies, when I serve the truth.

Half a century ago, I took my young man's body and my mind full of words to Berlin, to teach French to the Prussian king. He was Frederick, the "King in Prussia". I quickly realized the slur in his title, for beyond the borders of his own realm, Frederick was no king, but a nobody. When he was not expanding his kingdom at the mouth of a cannon, he was writing French poems and playing the flute. Quantz was his teacher of music and my responsibility was to correct His Majesty's horrendous grammar and give his verses some semblance of style. Then I had quipped to Quantz, "I am the French tutor of the German tooter." Quantz' laughter was as genuine as his advice was a chilling. "Most amusing, Monsieur, but His Majesty laughs only at his own jokes and we dutifully share in his merriment, no matter how painful." Such consideration for my indiscretion made me like the man who made the King's music.

It took me a while to appreciate the flute master, Johann Joachim Quantz. We would never be Johann and Charles, for such intimacy is both unsuitable and dangerous for servants in grand palaces. I would stand outside the music room, waiting to commence my duties, and be subjected to an hour or two of the royal repetitions. The sounds were excruciating and a stranger could be forgiven for thinking I was standing guard on a nest of mating cats. When silence relieved my ears, Quantz would appear calm and unruffled and exchange a few words. After many months, he trusted me with his exasperation and confessed that he "would not fit the whip to another's hand." I took this to mean that he would not allow his pupil to beat him, even if that pupil were the king.

I am grateful for his music. I can remember complex and delicate figures and now they calm me, when first they were just an annoyance. That was the true magic of Maestro Quantz.

Chapter 1

Candle Dancing

Quantz sat close to the kitchen table, hoping that Stefan could solve their problem. Anna held the candle in firm and practiced fingers, confident that a master carpenter with Stephan's eyes could see what was hidden from her and her husband.

Quantz furrowed his brow and gazed along the flute lying on the table. He was losing patience with the infernal tube that would not reveal its flaws. He picked up the instrument and took it to pieces. His fingers gently grasped the head joint and he separated it from the other sections. He peered into the hole that would take the breath, shrugged, and placed it on the table. The next section was pierced by the three holes for the left hand of the player. It was shorter than the head joint and beside it, the tube appeared to be stunted. The third tube also had three holes drilled through its body and was even shorter. The player would use the right hand on this tube. Last came the foot joint. It was the smallest and sported one small lever which covered the seventh hole and was worked by the player's little finger of the right hand. When he placed each piece side by side, they formed an oblique line from tallest to shortest nesting together on the table. Quantz stared in growing annoyance at each of the four parts of the dismantled flute. They were like naughty children, defiant and sullen, before irate parents.

Stephan glowered at the four cylinders and picked up the left-hand piece. He examined the three holes Quantz had delicately drilled into the tube and aimed its end at the candle in Anna's steady grasp. He squinted as though looking through a telescope and his eye searched the bore for any imperfections. Quantz had smoothed the grain until the tunnel glowed with a steady stream of light. He lifted each of his fingers and observed the candle light shine from each hole. Stephan placed the tube beside the other three sections and crossed his arms over his chest in exaggerated aggravation.

Stephan had been commanded by Augustus, the King of Dresden, to "proceed immediately to the residence of our most esteemed and beloved cousin, Frederick, King in Prussia, and supply a new floor according to His Majesty's taste." A royal wish is the subject's command, so Stephan packed up his tools and suffered the bumpy journey to Potsdam, knowing that he must create yet another floor to please his masters' feet but not knowing where he would rest his head. Quantz and Anna had saved him much discomfort and even more money when they insisted that he stay with them. His old friends had come up in the world if they could offer him free lodgings. Quantz had recalled their happy times together in Dresden and sensed that beneath Stephan's gruff thanks there was genuine appreciation of their consideration.

"My Dear Quantz, this one's a real bastard." Stephan admitted.

"That's why we're asking you," Quantz replied.

Stephan smiled at the compliment to his skill and the suggestion that his parents had never bothered to consult a priest before his birth. Stephan picked up the second tube and slid his index finger over the holes, as if searching for something lost. "Everything feels right," he confessed to Quantz.

"The flute is made for His Majesty's use. The instrument must conform to the laws of both science and music. We must not modify the instrument to accommodate the royal fist," Quantz explained.

"Well, then. If we cannot have a new king, let us at least try to make a joyful noise," Stephan said.

Stephan dug his elbows into the kitchen table and watched Quantz join the two central sections. Stephan knew that Quantz would have turned the tubes on a lathe. He had watched Quantz' concentration at the lathe and had always been impressed by how he could taper the bore of the tubes so that, when they were joined, they formed a conical tunnel from headjoint to foot joint as delicate as it was precise.

The tubes had been fashioned to end in a plug, so that each section fitted snugly together. Quantz joined the two central tubes until all six holes formed a straight line. He twisted the headjoint slightly. The head joint's breath hole was now slightly out of line with the six finger holes of body. The flute could then be offered to the player's lips so more air could travel down the bore. It was such a cunning placement, but as with all his work, the simplest solutions were sufficient to solve the most complex of problems.

Quantz blew into the hole and pronounced, "This headjoint can be adjusted later. We must have the whole flute working before we make the necessary modifications."

He fingered the lever on the footjoint and it dutifully rose and fell to seal the hole with its little pad. He squinted and ran his eye along the flute to make sure all the holes were aligned and blew one note. With the little finger of his right hand he slowly depressed and released the brass key and listened for any subtle variations of sound.

Anna and Stephan listened to Quantz raise and lower all his fingers, teasing a scale out of the mute wood. Quantz would pause with a finger poised and listen to each note escaping from the holes. Anna watched Quantz play from note-to-note and saw the scowl form. She knew that she would have to stop them, if this experiment were not going to proceed all evening. Quantz cocked his head to a quizzical angle, blew a note, and turned an expert ear to the end of the flute. The key jumped under his first touch but then rose and fell into a slow but steady rhythm under his little finger.

After a few protracted breaths, Stephan could barely hear it. Quantz worked the key, and the sound became ugly. Stephan had to close his eyes before he could hear the jangled discord, but the sound became confused as Quantz tickled the notes from under the key. Now that he could finally hear it, the dissonance was as obvious to him as pieces of wood joined with the wrong grain. There was no flow and the two sounds were like obnoxious twins fighting over trifles.

Quantz poised the flute before his chin and asked, "You hear it?"

"Yes," Stephan answered. "Give me that footjoint."

Quantz pulled off the foot joint and placed it in Stephan's waiting palm. Stephan played with the key but its action was smooth to his touch. He pulled out the little brass pin that held the key firm as a hinge in a door. The key dropped into his hand and he placed it on the table with its retaining pin. His fingers searched the wood's grain for ridges, until his eyebrows raised in discovery. "It's in the hole."

He offered the foot joint to Quantz, who searched for the imperfection. "Are you sure?" he inquired skeptically.

"It's there," Stephan assured him. "I felt it. You just have to look harder."

Quantz was annoyed, more by his inability to see the problem than by Stephan's confidence that he had found it. He pointed the foot joint at the candle flame. Light flooded the tunnel, so he waved the foot joint to-and-fro before the candle to see the contrast of light and dark. Then he saw it lurking in the shadows. It was a tiny knot in the wood. A few fibers had grown into a hard whorl, a bump no bigger than an infant's fingernail. It was just enough of a blemish to make the key slightly hiss and flatten the note. Such a tiny defect could produce a clamor of surprising shrieks and disconcerting squeals.

"Excellent," Quantz exclaimed. "I'll take a file to that, later."

Quantz replaced the key, assembled the flute, and raised it to his lips. He sat aiming the end of the flute at the candle. Stefan rested his cheek on the table to watch how the flame behaved in the stream of air.

Quantz sounded one low and sustained note at the candle's flame. The little finger of burning tallow stood defiantly straight, and Quantz wanted to spank it. Stefan squinted at the mocking glow and sighed, "The sound will not travel." Stefan sighed in disgust, "Try it again."

Quantz sat poised to play, and his eyes waited for Stefan's signal. "This time, the lowest pitch," he said, and Quantz' fingers settled onto the six holes. He could feel the sharp edges of the newly drilled holes. After a few months of being played, the holes would blunt and soften to the touch. Stefan nodded and Quantz fired a single note at the candle. The smoke above the candle didn't waver. Stefan shook his head in frustration. Quantz leaned closer, blew a long stream of sound and gently waved the flute before the candle. The flame swayed like a befuddled drunkard wandering his way home.

The brightness filled the little kitchen, but the sound could barely stagger across the table. Anna stood waiting behind her husband, clutching a second candle.

Anna and Johann Quantz had spent many evenings voicing the flutes he made for their master. They called it candle-dancing and joked that they would always have a good supply of candles as long as Frederick kept playing the flute, no matter how badly. The house, the food, and the salary were only the most obvious benefits of Quantz' post as

Music Teacher to His Majesty, Frederick, King in Prussia. When the servants delivered racks of new candles, Anna claimed their future was bright. Quantz assured her that he would keep his pupil happy, even if he went deaf.

Stefan shook his jowls at Quantz. "Do it the way you play," he commanded. Quantz's chest bulged and he coaxed a swelling arpeggio from the tube. He passed the end of the flute back and forth before the candle, as if charming a snake. The flame almost guttered at the low notes, but when Quantz lifted his fingers and raised the pitch, the flame leaped in thrilling shudders. He marched his fingers slowly down the tube, and the flame grew drowsy, as from a lullaby. With the final note, Quantz cast a parting kiss, and the candle fell into a pungent sleep. They sat silent in the darkness, breathing the waxy perfume, until Anna lit a new candle.

When his eyes adjusted to the light, Quantz squinted critically over the oblong hole of the head joint. It was cut perfectly into the tube, angled to guide the player's breath down the bore. He blew one sustained note. "Do you hear it?" he asked Stefan.

"Again," Stefan answered.

Quantz sounded the note and Stefan strained to hear the slightest difference in tone.

Years before, Quantz had performed this same tuning operation and told Stefan to listen for the commas. Stefan had grumbled, "Are you playing music or punctuating a sentence?" Quantz answered the rebuke beneath Stefan's annoyance with a contemptuous scowl. "My Dear Master Carpenter and Royal Cabinet Maker," Quantz had pronounced, "commas are the slight variations in pitch around a note." The simple statement silenced Stephan's thoughtless wit. Quantz could hear distinct pitches where Stephan was deaf. Every note was like a cut of wood, but Quantz could see the furrows of each grain. It was then that

Stephan realized that Quantz could hear as a painter could see. His admiration conquered his frustration. Never again would he doubt his friend's wondrous ear.

"I can hear two," Stefan tentatively confessed.

Quantz blew again, until a clear and pleasant sound tickled Stephan's ear. "That's it," Stefan gasped, and Quantz knew the flute was tuned to the desired pitch.

Anna watched Quantz pull off the head joint, separate the two central tubes from the foot joint, and lay them side-by-side on the table. He examined the foot joint with resigned disappointment and placed it beside the other three tubes with its little key facing upwards. Anna thought the key was like the haughty noses of palace servants. She decided that this was the time to tempt them back to reality.

Quantz sat patiently listening to Stephan grumble over his work. He was to create a floor in the music room beautiful enough for a king's feet. He had his orders, but no indication of how he should proceed. He had to create something pleasing for his master, with the tacit threat that Stephan would pay if his work displeased. Quantz reassured him that it was the same with music. "He may give me a line of notes and I am to turn it into a masterpiece he can perform like a virtuoso." Stephan agreed that even if he wished to give satisfaction, there was not a hint of what would satisfy the royal expectations.

Anna put a stop to their useless complaints with a tray of apple tarts. "Now, put away the toys and eat like little boys." They laughed at her oft repeated gibe and eagerly spooned through the crust to release the steam of sweet cinnamon and tart fruit. Anna was proud that they so enjoyed something she had made with the simplest of ingredients. Their appetite was sufficient applause for her efforts.

They sat staring at the four parts of the flute resting neatly beside the scraped dishes of their treat. Each section had to work in concert with the others. If the parts did not cooperate, there would be no music. They all knew that a flute was just a tube of wood with holes bored into it. So many people made the mistake of thinking that the music was in the instrument, when it was in the musician. Only the musician gave it breath and life. Music had to be earned through long years of practice. It could not be bought.

Chapter 2

Serpent in the Garden

The front door slammed politely but insistently behind him. Quantz squared his shoulders and centered his wig for the morning walk to work through Potsdam. It was a short climb up the hill to the palace, but he dallied in his daily saunter to his duties. He loved the sounds of the shops opening and the rattle, and thump of tradesmen's tools was always a joy.

The baker bid him a cheery "Fair morning to you, Maestro." Quantz tipped his hat and cast a smile at the dough-dusty fingers waving to him from the mixing table. The blacksmith raised his head from his forge and hammered a ringing greeting on his anvil. The street cleaner ceased his rhythmic sweeping on Quantz' approach, so the dust cloud from his broom would not besmirch the coat of their music man. Quantz gloried in their unspoken compliments, for he knew this was not deference to his station, but respect for his person.

He had to admit that Potsdam was something of a wonder, a very defiance of Nature. When he had first visited Berlin, Potsdam was just a way-station where carriages stopped only for the most urgent repairs. Just another North German hamlet with barely a score of wooden dwellings huddled around a forge. Then Frederick decided to build his retreat on these hills.

Potsdam looked like it had been drawn with a ruler because it had. Each street lay perfectly perpendicular to the other. It was a grid surrounded by green fields and meandering streams. The houses were built, by royal decree, according to a Dutch design, and all were exactly the same.

Each house was issued with just enough bricks for two stories with the front doors symmetrically facing each other. A solitary linden tree stood before each door, rigid as a sentry. The allocation of windows reflected the king's concern that the sun would wake everybody at the same hour. Enough glass had been requisitioned for the windows to celebrate the royal generosity for maximum effect and minimal cost. Potsdam was a monument to Frederick's love for his people, but the windows convinced His Majesty's loyal tenants that Old Fritz was a bit of a miser. The houses were so quickly constructed that people called them Freddy's Mushrooms.

The regularity of Potsdam made Quantz laugh to recall the baker lying drunk in his drawing room. Quantz was awaked by snoring that was not coming from Anna. He carefully descended the stairs to find the baker lying on the drawing room floor. When Quantz finally shook the baker into consciousness, the man asked, "What are you doing here?" The baker believed that he was sleeping it off in his own house, and Quantz had difficulty convincing the drowsy tipster that he had wandered into the wrong house. The baker was more bemused than embarrassed but made sure that a few more pastries were delivered to Mrs. Quantz in appreciation of explaining to his wife where he had spent the night.

Quantz strolled along the ornamental paths that skirted the artificial lake that watered the gardens and orchards. He mounted the stairs climbing through terraces piled one behind the other. As his feet rose higher, the earth gave the impression that Nature was ascending the heights to meet Art's beckoning arms in the form of two grand marble staircases stretching forth from the wings of the palace. Quantz had seen such allegories of gardening in all the royal seats he had visited throughout Europe. Such noble extravagance was nothing extraordinary to him. But the orange trees planted in serried ranks on each terrace were a remarkable innovation. Just the scent of them said that Frederick could make his northern kingdom bloom with the wonders of the south. The king could bend even the climate to his will. He could also sell the fruit to every grateful courtier, eager favor seeker, and needy supplicant for an exorbitant price. Quantz called it sweet bribery, but conceded ruefully that Frederick had a good head for business.

His muscles strained to carry him over the last rise, and Quantz stood on the long marble platform which ran along the front of the building. He rested near the railing and waited to catch his breath before completing his journey along the terrace to the music room.

Quantz had frequently pondered the contrast between the town where he lived and the palace where he worked. Frederick had wanted his private residence on the hills overlooking Potsdam. Potsdammers joked that the palace was situated so they always had to look up to the king, who was always looking down on them. Quantz greeted such confidences with beaming eyes but silent lips, for he enjoyed the jocular defiance of his neighbors. He was careful to laugh with one lip.

The town may have been as regular as the staves he gouged onto blank sheets of paper, but the palace was a melody of flowing stones. The crown of the hill had been sliced flat to hold the sculpted rococo walls and the surrounding mounts had been shaved of trees to enhance the view. From his perch at the balustrade running along the gallery, Quantz could gaze past Potsdam to see Berlin, nestled in its perpetual cloud.

On a clear day, Berlin looked like it was receding farther into the distance. But here in his pleasure palace, Frederick could live free of the restraints of ceremony and ignore the worries of statehood. In his retreat, the king was safe from the demands of kingship in Berlin and as far away from his wife as decorum and geography would permit, so he named his pleasure house Sans Souci.

The hammering ceased in the music chamber behind him and Quantz turned to greet Stephan emerging through the open door, beating clouds of fragrant sawdust from his hair. Stephan reminded Quantz of a cat scratching at an imaginary flea.

"You're early?" he prodded.

"Have to get the floors done before the cabinets."

"Where are they?"

Stephan pointed to his forehead and assured Quantz, "Here."

"What? You still have to make them?"

"We have to sit together and devise something elegant that will hold all that the moldy music. I can make book cases all day, but music comes in so many sizes. I'll have to know the right dimensions before I pick up a saw."

"That will happen soon. I am organizing all the papers. We can easily fit the cabinets to the folios."

Stephan did not mention that his early arrival was to avoid Mrs. Quantz' foul temper. He valued their friendship and did not wish it wrecked by Anna's periodic tempests. Something had lit her fuse, so he hurried to the palace to avoid the explosion. Quantz' face revealed that the husband had not been as lucky as the lodger.

Quantz opened his mouth to plan their work, but a blast of sound smothered his words. Stephan leaned over the railing, so his ears could search for the shriek howling from below. "What the hell is that?" he demanded. As if to answer him, three notes blurted from the orange grove and hissed up to the terrace. Then an arpeggio arched up from the trees. "Is it hunting season?" Stephan demanded. Quantz bellowed to the trees, "Heinz! Bring that thing up here."

A young boy emerged from the arbor and mounted the stairs. As he ascended, he blew more notes through a long twisted tube and arranged them into a march. The boy played each beat of the tune in a stately rise from step to step, with more grace to his movements than music in his playing.

Quantz immediately recognized the tune as all the rage. There had been a bloody but victorious battle involving more dead Austrians and Saxons than Prussians in some place named Hohenfriedberg, a village as unmemorable as its name was unpronounceable. People believed that Frederick had pried a fife from a dead hand and composed the tune on the spot. Berliners had set their own words to the music, which left no doubt about Frederick's amorous preferences or his physical agility. Whatever the truth, the tune was heard everywhere, and Quantz lamented its ubiquitous melody. It was a worm blocking the ear with repetitious intrusions.

The boy reached the top step and brought the march to a juddering climax. He stood holding his instrument in proper military fashion, and bowed deeply to Quantz.

"Master Stephan, allow me to introduce you to Heinz, an aspiring performer on the serpent."

Stephan glowered quizzically at the long bent cylinder nestled over the boy's elbow. Four feet of pipe had been twisted into two opposing semicircles punctured by six holes and crowned with a large trumpet's mouthpiece. With big lungs and broad fingers, sounds could be coaxed from the tube, but with little assurance that the contraption would stay in tune. A novice could produce a noise resembling a cow giving birth. It was called a serpent and its only advantage was that it could be heard over a cannonade of artillery. Heinz's burning desire was to take his place and his serpent into the fifth rank of the regimental band.

Heinz heard well-heeled shoes tapping up the stairs, squirmed in search of an escape, and darted through the open door of the music chamber. Quantz quickly placed himself before the open door, and Stephan stood guard beside him. They looked at the round and bewigged head of a courtier rise over the first step to be followed by a full body wrapped in a blue velvet morning coat. The shoes scrunched towards them through a film of plaster dust. The owner of this finery demanded of Quantz, "Where is that little miscreant?"

"Ah, Baron Belfort," Quantz greeted. "May I introduce Master Stephan from Dresden? He is creating a masterpiece in parquetry on which his Majesty can stand while playing."

The Baron's eyes widened with shock and quickly narrowed into barely suppressed outrage at Quantz' insolence of formally introducing him to a tradesman. He tilted his nose, as if to smell his quarry. "I meant that wretched boy."

"Which wretched boy?" Quantz inquired with exaggerated solicitude. "There are so many of them these days."

"Heinz."

"I think I saw him headed to the kitchens," Quantz mused.

"An annoying child," the Baron grumbled. "I sent him to the chancellory for a ream of paper and he has simply disappeared."

"That is the way of boys," Quantz commiserated.

"I have promised His Majesty that I would present him with my thesis on his return. How is that possible without the best quality paper?"

"When do you expect His Majesty to return to us?"

"When he is victorious."

Belfort's nose pulled the corners of his mouth into a moist sneer. "I would remind you that my correct title is 'Your Excellency'"

"As soon as I see him, I will send young Heinz to attend upon Your Excellency."

Belfort turned on his heel and marched along the terrace towards the kitchens, savoring what he was going to do to the wretched boy, when he found him.

Stephan was glad to see the baronial behind disappear down the far steps.

"He's quite full of himself," Stephan said.

"The Baron enjoys his food. It keeps his tailor in trade creating even more expensive coats to dress the Baron's infinitely expanding girth."

Heinz stuck his head between Quantz and Stephan. He squirmed between the men and stood awkwardly near the terrace railing, eyeing the path to the kitchens and relieved to see the Baron disappear in the distance. Quantz took the serpent from Heinz and examined the mouthpiece.

"Take this to my house. I will file it when I return."

Heinz stood not knowing what to do.

"If you hurry, Mrs. Quantz will give you an apple tart."

Heinz beamed in anticipation but did not forget to say, "Thank You, Master" and skipped toward the stairs. He raised the serpent to his mouth and blasted out a lively hunting call. With a flourish he danced down the steps in time with his tune. The boy's coordination amazed Stephan. He was fascinated that those spindly legs could perform such delicate choreography while blowing that infernal horn, without falling headlong down the stairs. They watched Heinz trip lightly and surely on his way to his treat. Quantz smiled to think that the boy's enthusiasm for the pastry was what kept his instrument in tune. He would remember to tell Anna that one of her culinary temptations had produced a musical miracle.

Stephan rested his hands on his hips and laughed at the sight of the skinny boy with the big horn dancing down the palace steps with all the grace of a courtesan's minuet. He turned to Quantz to confess, "That's much better than His Excellency's farts."

Chapter 3

Apple Tarts

Quantz opened the front door, carefully silencing any betraying squeak. He was relieved that he had oiled the discordant hinges. Avoiding his wife's wrath had become an acquired talent, nurtured through long practice, for he loathed confrontation and hoped the day had evaporated the morning's temper. He had dallied at his duties at the palace to return home at dusk. The door swung just enough to reveal Anna sitting serenely at the table with one finger to her lips.

"What has happened?" he asked as he stepped into his house.

"We have a guest."

Anna's forefinger beckoned, and Quantz followed her into the kitchen. She pointed to the truckle bed beside the stove, where restful snores and satisfied grunts sang a duet from beneath a blanket. He wondered why their guest was not sharing a room with Stephan.

"Who is it?" he asked.

"That boy," Anna explained.

"What boy?"

"The starving boy you sent to me."

That afternoon Anna had stood beside the table, grasping the handle of her milk jug. She had never seen such an appetite. The boy must have hollow legs, for he was on his fourth apple tart and showed no sign of slowing down. She was thankful the baker had given her a baker's half-dozen. Heinz sat poised to finish them all.

"Heinz?" Quantz exclaimed questioningly.

Anna's finger guided him back to the dining room table, and he sat waiting in his perplexity, until Anna started her tale. "He showed up expecting the apple tart you had promised him?"

"Oh. Yes, I did say you would give him a treat."

"He ate all six."

"Well, boys need feeding."

"This one also fed on your supper."

"But why is he here?"

His full attention delighted Anna and she jumped into her adventures of the day.

"First, I had to get rid of the stink. His coat smelled like some dead animal, but peculiar. When I saw his shirt, it was enough to drag him to the baths. He was an hour in the tubs, and I had to send him back for another hour. He looked at the soap as if he didn't know what it was. I made the bath man grease the dirt off him. I wouldn't use that shirt even for floor rags, so I gave him one of yours."

"Mine?"

"You have plenty. It was only your fourth best shirt."

"Cuffs as well?"

"No. No cuffs."

This was all so unexpected. Quantz had feared returning home to the lion, but this motherly lamb confused him.

"You are very generous, My Dear," he whispered with a hint of jesting intrigue. "You would give him the shirt off my back."

She glanced at the mirthful lines at his eyes, returned a coquettish smirk, and said, "No. Just off the laundry line."

Quantz looked at the coat draped over two chairs and sucked in the musty perfume wafting from the material.

"I had to soak that in the rain barrel," Anna proudly complained. Quantz raised an eyebrow for her to continue. "It went into the water dull brown. It needed a second rinse and came out blue. Then, I had to wash it again." She nodded her chin and inquired, "What is it?"

Quantz examined the languishing garment more closely. He spread the lapels, moist to his fingers, to reveal the lyre emblazoned in raise stitches. "It's a musician's coat. A parade dress one. Only for ceremonial occasions."

"So, this Heinz is a musician?"

"No. He just blows on his infernal horn."

Anna was eager to share her discoveries and her queries. "But nothing fits the lad."

Quantz controlled his tongue, allowing Anna's speculations to tease him. He fingered the soles of a pair of stockings drying on the back of another chair. "These are for the servants of the Gentleman's Boudoirs," he mused aloud. He offered the heel of a single stocking. "Look." Anna rubbed the proffered stocking between expert thumb and fingers. "Never been darned," she exclaimed.

Quantz enjoyed their shared mysteries but was loathe to let their game end too soon. "Doesn't really make an ensemble of a costume," he said suggestively.

"Even the shoes," Anna responded. She picked up a pair of scuffed and cracked brogues from the floor and thrust them forth for examination. Quantz turned his nose away and listened to Anna's discoveries.

"They are different sizes."

"Are his feet deformed?" Quantz wondered.

"No. But one shoe is stuffed with straw."

She stood to take the shoes to the street door. As she returned to their puzzle, she assured her husband, "I'll take them to the cobbler in the morning. Maybe he can salvage them."

Quantz could see that tomorrow he would be missing one pair of shoes. It would be a fair price for Anna's calming enthusiasm. If she were fussing over the boy, she would not be pestering him about furniture.

"Then there are his pants." Anna said.

"What about them?"

"You'll see."

Anna tiptoed to the window seat and returned with her proof. She held up the pants for his inspection. "I have never seen anything like this," she said. Quantz knew what they were before she returned to her seat. He touched one leg and the rough weave of a horse blanket sparked long rejected memories. He looked squarely at his wife and told her, "They are trousers for a blacksmith."

"This is what they wear?" she demanded incredulously.

"They are heavy and thick," Quantz continued, "so sparks will not burn their legs at the forge or anvil."

"The boy is a blacksmith?"

"Just from the waist down. From the waist up, he seems to be a bandsman, or so the clothing says."

"But nothing fits."

"Actually, now, everything fits."

"But who would dress a child in such rubbish?"

"Not a child. A scavenger," he clarified.

"What do you know about him?" she prodded.

"Well, now that you ask, almost nothing."

"Surely he is a palace servant."

"He appeared a few weeks ago. He pops up everywhere. Always carrying his horn. I first thought he was one of Ratzleff's brats."

"I do not like that Ratzleff," Anna grumbled.

"Neither do I, but I don't have to suffer the noises of our illustrious Master of the Military Band of the Potsdam Guards."

"Is that his title?"

"It's the one he gave himself. Everybody else calls him the Farting Midget."

Anna strangled her mirth with a fist over her mouth, lest she wake Heinz in the kitchen.

Quantz waited, uncertain if he should share his apprehensions. Anna's eyes wanted more, so he waited until her fingers left her face to gesture for more.

"Ratzleff is nothing compared to Belfort," he admitted.

Anna face fell into concern, "The women do not like that Baron."

"The Baron's feelings are mutual."

"They avoid him."

"They are wise," Quantz said. "Anybody who can keeps a safe distance from Baron Belfort."

"Including the King?" Anna asked.

"He plays the Baron like a puppet. The Baron would kiss any titled hand that holds his strings."

"You would think the King would see through his games."

"He does. But the Baron is so arrogant he cannot see the King's games."

"But what of our guest?"

"Whoever he is," Quantz mused, "he has collected his apparel from different parts of the palace." Quantz pointed to the stockings, "Domestics." Anna followed his finger to the coat, "Regimental band." And with a palm opened to the pants, Quantz clinched his argument, "Stables."

Her eyes beamed clear with sudden understanding, and he basked in her admiration.

"Are you hungry?" she gently asked.

"I thought you had given away my supper to the deserving poor?"

"I saved you some sausage."

"And a tart?"

"Of course. Just one."

Anna went to the sideboard to retrieve a pewter plate with two sausages and a knife. She set the dish before him, with a smile. The sausages were his favorites. The knife meant there would be no ceremony of cutlery and he could relax and enjoy his meal without the tyranny of etiquette. Dining always took the pleasure out of eating. He delicately sliced through the sausage, so no tapping of the plate would wake their guest nor trouble the quietude of their evening. He ate the sausage slice straight from the blade and savored the tang of pepper and sage. His hunger slowly faded, but he chewed for the taste and to prolong their conversation.

Anna brought her sewing basket to the table and draped the coat over her knees. Quantz watched her thread a needle and prick the cuff with the point. She carefully attached a brass button to the center of the cuff, and as he worked his way through the second sausage, he watched her stitch a row of buttons. He was careful to swallow before asking her, "Why are you decorating that coat."

"Not decoration. Cleanliness. These will stop him from wiping his nose on the sleeve."

It was so simple and yet so elegant and with each pull of the thread, he remembered why he had first loved her. She had a tenderness that the years had glazed over. She was kind at heart, and he hoped these embers of happiness would flame again. This was not to be rushed, for all his years of playing had taught him that haste destroys joy.

His eyes followed her fingers, and in the last glimmer of evening, he saw their scarlet roughness. He quietly suggested. "This next flute may pay for the furniture."

She dare not look at him. She pulled the thread tight and whispered, "Can we afford it?"

He wanted to show her that she had won the battle. "Stephan has some well-seasoned wood. We will use two of the blocks for the flute and charge my royal apprentice double."

"Won't he know you are cheating him?"

"It is not cheating if he wants it, and I will make something so wonderful that he will neither refuse the instrument nor question the account."

"But he's such an old miser?"

"His purse is tight, only when he has to pay for others. He never counts the cost, when he wants something for himself."

"But he will find out," Anna objected, and Quantz heard the tremble in her tone.

"The instrument I make for him will be worth four times what he usually gets. Twice the fee will really be a half-price bargain."

"Are you sure?" she prodded.

"The account will go through the Treasury to the Chancellor as it always does. If there is any question about the bill, Old Fritz will be satisfied that he is cheating me."

He reassured Anna that the next contribution to the royal flute collection would add to her meagre household. She had long coveted the dressers in other women's houses and had almost given up hope of ever having one of her own.

"Stephan has also brought much more wood than he can ever use in making the floor of the music room."

"How can his floor make my dresser?"

"Very simply, and when he has finished your dresser, very beautifully." He waited for Anna to continue sewing the sleeve cuff.

"I spoke with Stephan today," Quantz continued. "He has a lovely design for a Dutch cabinet. It has many drawers for clothing and high doors over wide shelves to hold all the dishes you can desire."

"We don't need much to hold our dishes."

"Then we will make it even bigger and order more dishes from Delft."

She could not speak. She would have her dresser and it would be unique to her. She would brag how her wonderful husband could supply such marvels. She could almost feel her neighbors' jealousy, but she would be very considerate of their feelings in her graciousness. That would make their hair burn.

The happiness welled in her heart, and she needed to wipe the relief from her eyes. She put down the coat and raised herself to pace slowly to the sideboard.

Quantz knew she was feeling overwhelmed but refused to admit that he had capitulated to her desires. He expected neither kisses of gratitude nor effusive hugs, but he was very happy when she placed before him the last of the apple tarts.

The Memoir of Charles Defutois

Part the Second

Paris, Lazarette Prison,

July 25, 1794

Memory is not the chronicle of a life. It just makes some sense out of living.

I can recall the first time I saw Frederick in all his glory. He returned from one of his wars and the streets of Potsdam could not hold all the people welcoming their king. His people were dutiful in their greetings, which I doubt not were mainly sincere.

He had increased his kingdom with parts of Silesia, the property of other kings. Frederick's father, the infamous Wilhelm, was politely known as distracted in his mind. The people just said he was as crazy as a sewer rat. Wilhelm had once chased a Jew through the streets of Berlin and horsewhipped him for hiding from the royal temper. While beating the Jew almost to death, Wilhelm had shouted, "I am your king. You must love me."

It was a tradition that, on Wilhelm's approach, Berliners would fall to their knees, clasp their hands, and pray that, "The Lord God will lead you to heaven with a string." Wilhelm was so grateful for his pious subjects' joy that he had engravings commissioned depicting a happy God the Father pulling Wilhelm through the Pearly Gates, while hoards of his distraught people begged that their king remain with them just a little longer. Never once did Wilhelm realize that they hoped he would be hanged.

But more than the insolence of cowering Jews, it was the arrogance of monarchs that mortified Wilhelm. The other kings refused to acknowledge him a true king. They gave him the title "King in Prussia" and snubbed him as a bumpkin. Wilhelm had begged and whined to every crown, and made himself a laughing stock from Versailles to Dresden. His wife had warned him that bringing such suits of nobility was less than noble, but he wouldn't listen to her good sense any more than he would hear the entreaties of the Jew he was beating. He actually thought he could win affection with a cudgel.

Frederick had no such delusions. He knew exactly the uses of the stick. If people would not attend to the force of reason, then he would teach them the reason of force. Where the father had wheedled, the son invaded. When the father had requested, the son demanded surrender. This was his enlightenment.

Along with his kingdom, the son had inherited the rejections of his father. But Frederick did not entreat recognition from his royal peers; he conquered their territories. If they condemned him to be king only in Prussia, he would take their lands and make a bigger Prussia to claim his rights.

The concert of outraged kings demanded satisfaction. Frederick graciously received their indignant ambassadors and laughed at their appeals to law. He responded with his pistol. He instructed an ambassador to deliver the weapon to his master, with the express declaration that this was Prussia's custom and his law.

He created an army unknown since the days of Alexander the Great. Four-fifths of his country's wealth was spent on his military might, and all his cunning was devoted to using this power in the achievement of his ambitions. There was much truth in the jest that Prussia was not a kingdom. It was an irresistible machine with some land attached to an army.

Ah, the pageantry of the conquering hero. Frederick returned to Potsdam with blaring bands and marching regiments. I could hear their approach from many miles, and as they marched through the triumphal arch, the massed bands stopped to serenade us all. It was my first experience of Prussian music and I am glad that it did not permanently deafen me.

The day was as cheerful as the sunlight was welcome, and the recollection brings warmth to this, my stoney accommodation.

Chapter 4

Triumphal Arch

Potsdam thrilled to the return of the king, his army, and their men. The families filled the streets, shuddering in expectation. Mothers struggled to let their children feel the excitement of the parade and to keep them safe from the cannons' wheels with a maternal slap. The regiment of the Potsdam Guards would be the last part of the parade, for the rest of the army would have already arrived at their barracks in Berlin.

Quantz and Anna stood at their front door, sharing the tingle of a thousand hearts. They were glad that the war had been as short as it was successful, for the fruit of victory was the predictable regularity of the peace. While the king was on campaign, the town had become accustomed to the stillness that settled even in the trees, and some were growing bored with the absence of the court. When the palace was thrumming, there was always interesting gossip. Even Potsdammers had difficulty finding scandal in an empty house, try as they might.

Anna gazed down the street and pulled inquiringly on Quantz' sleeve. "That's a new face," she observed. Quantz peered in the direction of her nod and raised an eyebrow. "Under the second tree," she prodded. He squinted into the distance, but was no further enlightened. "He is wearing a blue French coat." The color and the cut of the cloth immediately identified Anna's target. He returned a casual whisper. "That's Defutois," he said.

"And just what is a Defutois?" she grumbled.

"Something new, from Paris."

"Yet, more French fashion?"

"This one speaks. He is the new secretary to the king."

"Aren't there enough Germans?

"This one is rather special. He is to assist His Majesty with all things French."

Anna pasted a sly grin above her chin. "Doesn't he have Italians for that?"

Quantz answered with a knowing shrug and the hint of an arched brow. "This Frenchman is to correct all of the correspondence in that language, but only for the royal person."

The bands were approaching, scattering blaring triumph before them into every quarter of the town. The closer they came, the louder they played, until every house and all the pavements were soaked with anthems of martial glory. Quantz tapped his foot in time to their ridiculous march, repeated without pause or variation, as if he were listening to a finger circling a wine glass and hoping it would break. He looked at Drum Major Ratzleff leading the band with a stick taller than his head. The man looked as ridiculous as he was vain, but Quantz hoped that he was musical enough to keep Heinz out of his noisome gaggle of squeaking fifes and braying trumpets. "He looks confused," Anna said.

"I can think of no better description for Ratzleff's perpetual condition," Quantz jested.

"No. The Frenchman."

Quantz gazed down the street and admitted that Anna was right. "This is probably all very new to him."

"We should be good neighbors and invite him over."

"Well, that would be nice. Go get him."

"No. You get him. You can speak the French with him."

Quantz knew an order when Anna hinted and wove his way through the crowd to where Defutois stood in rigid perplexity. Anna watched them speak and soon Quantz was leading their new acquaintance to her. She could not understand the words, but Quantz' tone was inviting. She was grateful that he could be so courteous to everybody, for she had learned to hold her tongue and let him deal with people. Quantz was introducing them, and when she heard the Frenchman's name, she made a little curtsey and gave him a welcoming smile. The Frenchman was asking Quantz something, and when Quantz fell silent, the Frenchman returned the bow so low that Anna could smell the perfume in his wig. She wanted to be part of the conversation, so she mimicked drinking from a cup and saucer. Quantz gabbled again, and the Frenchman bowed a second time. Anna was feeling very much the mistress of her little palace but panicked when she wondered if she had enough coffee for three cups. She had heard that Voltaire drank forty cups a day, but assured herself that the French use small cups and decided that she could serve them all. After all, Voltaire was a notorious braggart. She stood watching them speak and grinned in her most relaxed manner to make the Frenchman feel welcome.

"Is there always such a parade?" Defutois asked.

"This is a special display and heralds His Majesty's triumph," Quantz explained.

"The music is so loud."

"It gets worse."

As if on cue, Defutois saw Ratzleff lift his mace and the band exploded in volume, if not in tune. Quantz watched Defutois wince and complimented him on being so musical. They turned their heads to see a matched team of six white horses struggle to haul an open carriage up the rise. The street erupted into mighty cheers as a prelude to the appearance of the King. Between the band and the crowd, Defutois was deafened, but his eyes strained to take in every detail of this, his first sight of Frederick, King in Prussia and his new master.

Frederick was smaller than Defutois had imagined. His head and shoulders barely rose higher than the sides of the carriage and the image reminded him of a small boy in a bathtub. Frederick sat quietly ignoring the crowd and graciously accepting the adulation that was his right. Defutois was struck with the thought that one's opinion of the scene depended on one's view of the subject. His Majesty could be both regal and absurd at the same time. His attention turned to two small grayhounds which bounded from seat to seat in the carriage. One would jump to Frederick's lap, imploring a pet with an insistent snout while the other leaned over the side snarling at the crowd and barking to imaginary foes threatening his master. The dogs changed places and Frederick became more animated by their tails wildly slapping their sides than the throng of wellwishers celebrating his safe return. Frederick looked directly at Quantz and ordered the coachman to stop.

"Are you well, Quantz?" he asked with sincere indifference.

"I am extremely well, Your Highness, now that you have returned to us as safe as you are victorious," Quantz replied and bowed stiffly but not deeply.

Defutois was flustered but decided to follow Quantz' example and bowed low to the carriage. His face blushed embarrassed infusions when he saw both his hat and his wig fall to the ground in front of him. Frederick looked amused by the shaven head bent in obeisant homage. One of the dogs, seeing easy prey in the wig was about to pounce out of the carriage, but Frederick giggled as he restrained the animal by the scruff of its neck. Frederick ordered the coachman to proceed and laughed heartily as the dog whined in disappointment.

As the coach continued, Anna grabbed the hat and wig and jammed both onto Defutois' sweating pate. He rose quickly and mouthed "Merci" to Anna. Quantz stood rigid, more to control his merriment at the scene than out of deference to the royal presence.

"If you are going to bow that low, you will need a better wig," he jibed.

"I am uncertain as to the customs here," Defutois admitted.

"Think of us as amusing but possibly dangerous barbarians," Quantz advised. "Just observe and follow what we do. You will find that we are too addicted to pork to be cannibals."

Defutois smiled in gratitude and performed the one-quarter bow as Quantz had done. His chin was no lower than the middle of his chest, and Anna giggled to hear his smothered question, "Like this?"

Quantz raised Defutois by the shoulders and assured him, "That's about right but you will improve with practice. No doubt you will have many opportunities to bow and scrape and soon you will be most proficient."

Defutois realized just how ignorant he was of court etiquette but he also knew that Quantz could initiate him into the subtle mysteries of being a favored servant in a royal household.

No sooner than the King's carriage proceeded out of sight than the regiments of the Potsdam Guards came into view. They marched in columns of companies in line. Each file of twenty men filled the street. Every soldier's face stared in determined concentration before them as they marched determinedly through the tunnel of cheering voices and waving arms.

Defutois was astounded by the sight. In France, a parade was a cavalcade of gesturing and posing individuals where every foot soldier and rider vied for the attention of the people. Before him passed serried ranks of completely uniform units. When one file passed before his vision, the soldiers were so even that he could see only one until they moved on their way. Each soldier held his musket at exactly the same angle and each musket glinted a brilliant line of sharp bayonets. Every foot touched the ground at the same time, so that he had the odd sensation that he was looking at some gigantic animal whose hundreds of feet rose and fell as one.

Quantz heard Ratzleff order the band to play that infernal ditty that was all the rage. The tune would not be all that bad if it were not so regular. He wanted to cry out and pen some variation to the line of notes, but that was impossible. Devoid of modulation or even simple harmony the jingle could be hummed by a drooling idiot and quickly became as stale as curdled milk. But he comforted himself with the thought that there is no accounting for taste, especially with those who have none. He improvised some lyrics to distract him from the melody, "They marched to the beat of a thrilling martial tune. Their feet stomped the cobblestones and echoed down the street." The tune was appropriate to a soldier's needs for it had the regularity of a mill wheel and the steadiness of a cow resigned to its slaughter.

Defutois saw Anna pull at Quantz's sleeve and point to a woman pushing herself through the crowd. The woman shoved herself through an opening and walked back down the hill in the opposite direction to the soldiers. Anna was counting in German, but Defutois knew enough to link Anna's gestures to the woman. Another woman fell out of her place to follow the first woman, and Anna continued her count. Defutois presumed that the women were servants and that they had to return to their duties before the parade ended. He was confused by Anna's counting on her fingers and Quantz' head nodding in grave agreement. Whatever this was, it was more serious than a pair of scullery maids hastening to their sinks. When the third regiment marched by, a shriek erupted from the pavements and more women joined the procession down the hill. Defutois surmised there was some connection between the segments of the parade and the behavior of these women.

At the passing of the fourth regiment, the trickle burst into a flood, but this time, the women were joined by old men and many children. He finally asked for enlightenment from Quantz, who stood tall but with a rigid face. "Where are those women going?"

"They are hastening to Berlin?"

"Is that where the parade ends?"

Quantz resigned himself to an explanation he did not want to admit. "When the army returns, the parade tells us who will not be returning. If the women do not see their husbands in the ranks, they run to the barracks in Berlin in the hope that he will be among the wounded."

Defutois immediately apprehended the significance of the two parades moving in opposite directions. He looked to Quantz in barely restrained shock. Quantz inclined his head, as if sharing an amusing confidence. "In France, you win battles. In Prussia, we win wars. They are very expensive."

He was cut off by Anna's shaking finger and exclamation, "There goes the baker." Defutois watched a man sprinting through the crowd. The people parted as the Red Sea of old and he ran through them to some far shore of desperate hope. "He will be looking for his son," Quantz said. "If he is not at the Berlin barracks, they will never meet again in this life."

Quantz scowled and commanded, "We need some of Anna's wonderful coffee." He turned to their door and they followed him into the house.

Defutois sat at the table amid the clutter of empty cups and saucers, wishing to understand all he had seen that day. Quantz was happy to instruct him, but was careful to remind the Frenchman that his future at the palace could be as short as the men on campaign. Quantz was equally determined to help this foreigner, for he judged the new man both worthy of and desperate for his advice.

"When you are with the King, remember that he wishes to be informal," Quantz said.

"Informality and royalty do not mix," Defutois observed.

"Here, informality means that you bow in a slightly relaxed manner. This allows the king to imagine that his subjects love him so much that they are at their ease in his presence."

"It may take some time for me to learn this."

Anna started to talk, but Defutois was perplexed and his eyes appealed to Quantz. "My wife would like to scalp you."

"What?"

"She wants your wig."

Defutois obeyed with the assurance that the lady of the house was not a howling savage. He removed his wig and offered it to her. Quantz rested his chin on his palm and his elbow on the table, enjoying Defutois' apprehension and curiosity.

Anna grasped the wig's queue, raised her arm over her head, and beat the wig against the table, as if she were dispatching some aggressive rodent. Talcum powder rose to their faces, as she pounded Defutois' ornate toupee. Quantz laughed at Anna thoroughly enjoying the beating she was giving her table. "You must use much less powder in your coiffure. His majesty has a sensitive nose."

Anna offered the wig to Quantz and they thoroughly inspected the rows of deftly braided wool. Quantz read a label glued to the inside of the wig's skull cap and asked, "Who is LaFontaine?"

"Monsieur LaFontaine is the Master Perruquier to His Majesty. Everybody at Versailles wears a LaFontaine," Defutois proudly explained.

Anna queried Quantz, "Perruquier?" and he told her, "This LaFontaine is a high-class wigmaker." Anna looked at the wig with increased respect and rubbed her thumb and forefinger before Defutois' face. He turned an inquisitive cocked head to Anna, who simply said, "How much?"

Defutois was shocked. No Frenchman would ever think of asking the cost of fashion. Although he was astonished by Anna's interest in money, he could see that she was eagerly waiting for the answer. But he was also determined to understand the strange manners of these people who had been so kind to him. He raised two fingers in response.

"Two what?" Quantz asked.

"Two Louis d'Or," Defutois responded simply.

Anna had no need of a translation for she was fluent in all of the currencies of every kingdom. Her fingers savored the quality of the wig and her eyes shone approval at Defutois.

Quantz sniffed the air. "You will have to stop using perfume."

"Is the aroma offensive?" Defutois asked.

"The scent will remind the King of the denizens of the Faubourg Sainte Denis," Quantz proclaimed.

Defutois immediately saw that Quantz knew of Paris' notorious brothel district and was warning him that the King also knew about such places. It would be safer not to mention the female trades.

Anna was fussing around Defutois. She was armed with a needle and thread and offered him the wig, as if it were her most recent kill. Quantz told him to put it on as he usually does and sit still. Defutois obeyed and felt Anna's hands on his back. Quantz smiled at his discomfort. "It is an old trick

Anna invented. She sews the braid of my wig to the back of my collar, so that it will not fly off when I bow."

Defutois laughed at this simple subterfuge and surrendered to Anna's expertise. She beckoned him to stand and turn around. Quantz continued with his tutelage. "When you remove your coat, first push back the wig. When you put on the coat, pull the wig back onto your head. That way, it will stay where God and Monsieur LaFontaine placed it, on your head."

"I can only thank you for this advice."

"When you bowed so low, the king did not see your face. He would remember you always as 'that idiot who can't control his hair,' if there would be any repeat performance of the flying hairpiece."

Defutois removed his coat, and spread it over the back of his chair with the wig dangling from the collar. Anna gestured over Defutois' body and seemed to be complaining about something to Quantz. Quantz nodded sagely and launched into a lecture. "Let's look you over."

Defutois stood for inspection. "The trousers are very well cut, but make sure you have two buttons holding the cuffs just below the knee."

"Is that really necessary?" Defutois inquired.

"Only if you do not wish to look ridiculous when one button pops open and your stocking falls to your feet."

Anna stroked her chin and contemplated Defutois feet.

"You have a very fine shoemaker,"

"Yes, he is in Paris and knows all the latest fashions."

"That is good. His Majesty has a peculiar interest in shoes."

"He follows fashion to the heel?"

"And the toe. He wishes to see his own face when he looks at your footware."

"These shoes are scuffed but they are clean."

"Cleanliness may be next to godliness but brilliance is dear to royalty. You must shine them."

Anna gestured for him to take off his shoes. She left them on the floor beside the table and retreated to the kitchen. "Anna will ensure that you are properly attired for your first meeting tomorrow. Follow her directions and all will be well."

Anna returned with a plate and one sausage. She sat down close to Defutois, thrust her left hand into the shoe, and attacked the toe with her right hand and the sausage. Defutois had never seen anything like this. Anna pressed the sausage and smeared the fat into the leather. Her fingers thrust more fat into the welt and she gave special attention to the heel and the sole. Soon, both shoes glistened with a coating of meaty grease and he could barely distinguish between the shoe and the sausage.

Quantz gazed over the table and nodded approval to his wife. Defutois waited until Anna offered him a towel. He started to rub his shoe, but Quantz restrained him. "Leave them like this overnight. In the morning polish them to a high sheen and you will be a pretty dish to set before a king."

Anna smiled her approval at Defutois and he bowed to her with a most sincere, "Merci, Madame." Quantz and Anna laughed at their guest's eagerness to learn their ways and his willingness to show his appreciation of their care. Quantz turned to Defutois' smiling face and told him, "I do believe you are ready to be thrown to the dogs."

Chapter 5

Belles Lettres et Bon Mots

Defutois waited at the entrance to the music chamber. A skinny boy led him through corridors and up and down stairs until Defutois was thoroughly confused. The child had insisted on telling him stories of every door they passed, complete with lurid descriptions of what happened behind those closed doors, until Defutois surrendered in silence to his jabbering guide. The boy assured him that he, Heinz, would be waiting for him to lead him back to his quarters and disappeared. Defutois stood with growing apprehension and felt like a forgotten grenadier who could never abandon his guard post for fear of punishment.

Squeaks and grunts seeped under the door and pricked his ears. The duet of creaking notes signaled that Quantz was about to finish the royal music lesson. Defutois relieved the melange of apprehension and boredom by examining his face reflected in his shoes.

He had followed Anna's orders and smiled to think that Germans used their ubiquitous sausages for everything. He had burnished his shoes with a kitchen rag and now his feet were enveloped in a vibrant sheen. His silver buckles were less brilliant than the leather. He had to admit that each step was a shimmering trail on his luminous passage.

The sounds abruptly stopped, the door opened, and he saw Quantz' back emerge through the opening. "Until our next hymn to Cecelia, Your Majesty," Quantz spoke into the room. Defutois watched Quantz silently close the door and spin on one foot to face him. "Ah, Defutios," he greeted. Quantz looked over the Frenchman, and his eyes lingered on the shoes. "I took your gracious suggestion," Defutois amitted. The vaguest hint of approval beamed from Quantz' eyes. "You'll soon discover the many uses of the simple sausage," Quantz quipped through lips pulled almost to a sneer.

Quantz' head nodded to the door. "There is no need to knock. He is waiting for you and he does not like too much ceremony on an entrance." Defutois gave a short bow, as much to acknowledge the instruction as to assure Quantz that he was practicing his gestures in the Prussian style.

"The exit is a different matter," Quantz continued with more seriousness. "You walk backwards until you are through the door. Never turn you back on the Royal Presence on your exit."

Quantz's steps echoed down the corridor and faded through a distant door, leaving Defutois in his trepidation. He stared at the door, gulped a chestful of courage, and entered.

Frederick looked up from his desk and rose to greet his new tutor. "Ah, Monsieur Defutois," Frederick exclaimed, mustering his curiosity into a resemblance of sincere informality.

Defutois did not know the protocol of response and stood gaping like a village idiot. Frederick immediately recognized the fluster of silence and asked, "I trust you have had a not too unpleasant journey to our domains?"

"The journey was shortened by the destination," Your Majesty."

Frederick caught the subtlety of the compliment lurking behind the words. "Spoken like a true Frenchman."

Defutois waited and felt his nervousness flow out of him like low tide. He had never met any royal person and wondered if they all had this talent to disarm their subjects.

"Your journey was preceded by the highest recommendations of the most distinguished minds of your country."

"I am honored, Sire," and Defutois performed his most accurate mimicry of a bow.

Frederick smiled to see both ease and discomfort in his newest servant. The best tactic was a leading question wrapped in a considerate command. Asking for a response in conversation was just like a probing attack, and Frederick was the master of both.

"I am curious to know your opinion on the living authors who write the French language with the greatest correctness," he asked with genuine interest.

Frederick gave Defutois a moment's pause to collect his thoughts and demanded, "Tell me about them."

"D'Olivet, d'Alembert, Buffon, are all masters of both grammar and style. I would not hazard an opinion of the content of their works. That is bet left to the judgement of Your Majesty."

The deference to Frederick's opinions, whatever they were, flattered his vanity and Defutois was emboldened to end the list with the name of Jean Jacques Rousseau. All familiarity immediately flushed from Frederick's body, and Defutois was threatened by his outraged stare.

"Rousseau is a madman," Frederick proclaimed. Defutois stood like a rabbit before a snake and waited. "I offered the man asylum in my states, a pension of two thousand livres, and a comfortable house in Pancow beside the magnificent gardens of Schonhausen." Frederick paused, as if his list was sufficient reason to explain Rousseau's insanity.

"The offer is as generous as it is gracious, Your Majesty."

Frederick stomped to his desk and returned, offering Defutois sheets of paper. Defutois' finger felt the creases where the papers had been squeezed by an angry fist and later smoothed by calmer fingers. "And this is how that charlatan has returned my generosity." Defutois was shocked by Rousseau's response and relieved by Frederick's command to "Read it aloud."

Defutois stretched his back to declaim the letter, "Your Majesty offers me asylum, and promises me liberty. But you have a sword and you are a king: you offer a pension to me who never did you a service, but have you bestowed one on each of the brave men who have lost either a leg or an arm in doing your service?" Defutois was silenced by such outrageous insolence.

His attention was taken by the two dogs who came sniffing at his legs. Frederick watched the dogs circle and there was no smile. One dog raised two paws to Defutois' thigh and sniffed intently. Frederick watched the trio carefully, interpreting their movements. When the dog's tail swished casually, Frederick's eyes gleamed and he assured, "He wants his head scratched." Defutois offered three fingers and was met with reassuring licks. The other dog's muzzle examined Defutois' feet and slumped into a begging quiver. Frederick watched the animals intently, observing every swaying tail and friendly yelp. "Despite what such illustrious writers have said about you, Monsieur, Tommy and Little Kelly would have the last word, if they could talk."

"They are most expressive and I would expect nothing else from such an eloquent master."

Frederick bellowed and the clouds disappeared from the room. "I would like you to see the riposte I have prepared for the Lunatic of Geneva." Frederick offered another sheet of paper. "Would you be so kind as to help with the style and the proper expression to such a missive?"

Defutois quickly scanned the sheet. The verbs were in the wrong place for a Frenchman but perfectly in order for a German sentence. The thoughts were mature and complex, but the tenses were as simple as any school boy's scribblings.

Every smudged character was an assault on Defutois' taste and a challenge to his discretion.

Defutois pointed to Frederick's letter. "Your Majesty may consider changing this word in the salutation." Frederick peered at his writing and his brows steepled into a question. "What is wrong with that word?" he queried.

"The word is common to a barrackroom but not appropriate for a palace."

"But I have heard this word many times."

"On a parade ground?"

"Well, yes and with my friends. What is its nuance in French?"

"It is the female organ of generation."

"Excellent. For that is exactly what such an ungrateful wretch deserves."

Frederick kicked a chair to his desk. The dogs flashed their ears in anticipation of some excitement, but slumped to the floor when they saw their master sit. Frederick picked up a pen and sucked on the nib. He looked back at Defutois and pointed to the empty chair he had just assaulted. "Sit here and we can both devise a better answer."

Defutois sat at Frederick's side and relaxed into the irresponsibility of a servant. The master, like his dogs, had the last word, even if that word would bar him from polite society.

Frederick straightened his back, as if jolted by a new thought. "If you can not speak German, how did you get from France to Berlin?"

"By a most fortunate acquaintance and traveling companion, Your Majesty."

"Monsieur, in this room, we dispense with the usual ceremonies. Too many, "Sires" and "Your Majesties" interrupt the flow of thought."

Frederick's silence was a command to continue.

"The coach was shared with one of your officers, a most gallant gentleman from Savoy. This captain was in your service and was wounded six times. He related to me how he had been taken prisoner in the city of Dresden, bleeding and almost completely naked in the dead of winter. My companion translated for me at every stop on the way and the brilliance of his conversation shortened the journey."

"What is the name of this captain?"

"Favrat, Your Ma… Favrat." Frederick's eyes narrowed at the name. Defutois was trapped by his own anecdote, but Frederick's manner demanded more. "The captain was particularly eager to know if the disasters occasioned by war had been repaired in Dresden."

"Particularly, Dresden?"

"Yes, Your Majesty." and Defutois bit his lip at the slip of the title of honor.

"And what did you tell him about the repairs in Dresden."

"I was unable to tell him anything because I have never been to Dresden either before, during or after the war."

"You meet such curious people in coaches," Frederick reminisced, "especially when they are soliciting information on the fortifications of a conquered city. You did well to remain silent."

Defutois didn't know if Frederick could see the sweat welling under Dufutois' wig. He now understood why his carriage companion had taken such an interest in the walls of Dresden. Clearly, this Favorat was a spy, seeking the most recent intelligence concerning repairs to the fortifications, the same walls which Frederick had knocked down on his campaign. He felt a fool at not recognizing the obvious.

Frederick mused for a moment and asked, "You are not acquainted with the German language?"

"No, but I soon hope to be master of it."

"I advise you not mean to learn it."

"Would not mastery of German be of invaluable service in my duties in the French language, so as better to serve Your Majesty's desires?"

"You would find that you would soon contract the habit of uttering the same Germanisms as we do. You would not be able to resist the contagion of words which fall from our lips in speaking French."

Defutois was wondering how a knowledge of German would contaminate his French. Frederick seemed to think that one language could infect another with a grammatical pox.

Enjoying Defutois' obvious confusion, Frederick explained. "It would be impossible for you to preserve the pure taste and exquisite relish of the beauties, the subtle refinement, and genius of your native language."

Defutois lifted his head as if he comprehended the hidden wisdom of the last statement, even though it all sounded like nonsense.

Frederick observed Defutois' flustered eyes but was also relieved to see Defutois defer to his logic.

"It accordingly follows," Frederick charged in with the conclusion, "that in proportion as you contract our manner of speaking, you will imperfectly fulfill the duties that are the object of your embassy to this country."

Frederick was determined to start their relations as he meant them to continue. He would accept no position other than the knowledgeable master and Defutois would find defense only as the appreciative servant.

"Therefore," Frederick pronounced, "in your quality of a gallant man, earnest to accomplish well your vocation, I require you to give me your word of honor that you will not learn our language."

There was left open the suggestion that learning German was tantamount to betrayal of both France and Prussia.

Defutois perceived that displeasing the king was the essence of treason. He would keep his ears open twice as much as he would keep his mouth shut.

"You have my word, Your Majesty."

Frederick did not correct him but turned and addressed the door behind him. "Monsieur le Catt," he commanded, and the door opened as if it heard "Open Sesame." The frame was filled by a man almost as wide as he was tall. Frederick softly said to the apparition, "See to it that Monsieur Defutois has everything he requires to fulfill his duties and to amuse his person." The man responded, "Immediately, Sire," and deftly from long practice, shut the door with his foot as he bowed his way out.

"Until our next pleasant meeting," Frederick complimented and his eyes indicated the door .

Defutois followed the advice of Quantz and the example of le Catt and bowed himself out of the royal presence.

He didn't know whether to be relieved or surprised to see Heinz leaning against a wall and picking his nose. Heinz snapped to attention and nodded for Defutois to follow him. They wormed their way through the central corridors until Heinz opened a door to the terrace.

Defutois's agitation calmed when he saw Quantz dallying over the balustrade. Quantz straightened at the sound of Defutois' footsteps and exclaimed, "I see you have met with His Majesty's approval."

"Then you know something I don't." he sighed. "A large man answered the summons."

"That is Baron von Clodtz," Quantz said. "He is the Marchal of the Palace, the Major Domo of the royal toilette, His Majesty's Exchequer of the Home Finances, but more importantly, our paymaster."

"He is a huge fellow," Defutois, lost for words, spluttered.

"He has grown into all the titles and orders bestowed upon him. He is so fat, so he can wear all his medals."

"So he is the power behind the throne?"

"There is only one power and it seldom sits, except to ride to battle." Quantz looked to Berlin's smoking chimneys in the far horizon and casually asked, "What about the royal menagerie?"

"The dogs were all over me."

"In that case, may I be the first to congratulate you on the confirmation of your new post as Master Grammarian of the Chamber."

Defutois now understood the purpose of Anna's attention to his shoes. Her efforts and all his rubbing were not just for the king to see his face. It was her strategy so the dogs could smell the meat.

"Because of the dogs."

"Let us just say that an Italian dog can be tamed by a German sausage."

Chapter 6

Quack

The music chamber was much too small, too intimate, for such an august assembly, so the grand salon had been prepared to receive the King's distinguished guest from France. Dozens of chairs formed a semicircle to accommodate notables of Frederick's Academy of Sciences. The dining tables had been moved to the walls and laden with refreshments for both the stomach and the tongue. Frederick was peculiarly republican concerning the instruction and betterment of his minions, so he had ordered all the doors and windows to be opened for the court servants. All the palace's workers and retainers had been invited to stand along the terrace and gaze in astonishment at their master's most recent enthusiasm. The higher courtiers sat in a cloud of discreet chatter while the terrace bubbled with rowdy indifference. Quantz and Defutois stood at the very back of the salon close to the window where Stephan and Heinz perched in uncertain expectation.The far end of the salon was reserved for two mysterious structures, hidden under draped sheets. They resembled statues waiting patiently for their unveiling.

The occasion of all this excitement was the visit of M. Jacques de Vaucanson, the Genius of Lyons. For many months, Frederick had been begging Vaucanson to attend his court. He had offered his sincerest admiration for Vaucanson's scientific achievements, flattered the inventor's famous vanity, but finally, the offer of a generous fee, complete with all traveling expenses, had enticed the Master of Mechanics to Berlin. When he received Vaucanson's gracious reply, Frederick was in fits of impatience. He had even ordered a regiment of hussars to meet the man at the border and escort him and his precious cargo all the way to the palace. No one had reported Vaucanson's reaction to this military guard, but he was sufficiently impressed by the blandishments of royalty to transport his machines across an entire continent to entertain a king.

Some of the royal entourage were sufficiently close to Frederick to snort in derision at the very mention of Vaucanson's name, but the king dismissed all their warnings that the Frenchman was nothing more than a clever charlatan. Others pointed to the gross expense of his contraptions, but they knew there was always just enough in the budget to appease the royal desires. The Chancellor noted that the cost was greater than the budget for the arsenal, and this gave Frederick pause just long enough to calculate that one of Vaucanson's marvels was no more expensive than twenty cannon. The Chancellor and the Treasurer fell silent and filled the void with cheerful deference to His Majesty's superior command of accounting.

Quantz and Defutois stood as the very back of the assembly in the places allocated to only the most favored servants, but they had an excellent view of the proceedings over the heads of the collegiate, nodding sagacious approval of the forthcoming lecture.

Defutois had only encountered such a collection of talent at one royal levee at Versailles and asked Quantz to identify each genius.

"Who is the rotund gentleman at the very front?" he asked.

Quantz cast a casual eye to the seats reserved for the most celebrated scholars.

"The bespectacled man wearing that beaver hat?" Quantz queried.

"Yes. He looks familiar."

"That is because you have probably seen his image in France. No doubt in one of the King of France's warrants for his arrest. That is the renowned, if not infamous, M. Pierre Louis Moreau de Maupertuis."

"The Maupertuis, the famous explorer?"

"The very same. Also, mathematician, homme des belles lettres and, according to your king, international scoundrel."

"But Maupertuis actually established the true shape of the earth."

"Correct. His expedition to Lapland proved that the globe is shaped like a squashed pumpkin and disproved the theory that it is a giant carrot."

Defutois now felt honored to be in the same room as such a mind, even if he recalled that Maupertuis had absconded with the money the king had given him for another expedition. Maupertuis had made his trip to Prussia on a pretext of further research and accepted Frederick's offer to be his Director of the Prussian Academy of Sciences. The French were outraged at this betrayal, so Frederick salved Maupertuis' conscience with an increased salary. It was then that Defutois remembered that the family of Maupertuis were notorious and successful pirates from St. Malo.

"You, if anyone," Quantz quipped, "should appreciate that His Majesty's taste runs to the French in all things. He even has a French sous-chef who creates culinary wonders from the flanks of horses and the legs of frogs."

Count Belfort pranced into the salon and the courtiers quickly made a place for him. Heinz watched the performance of fake bonhommie, glowered at the Baron's back shuddering in amusement, and stuck his tongue. Stephan quickly slapped the young rascal's tongue back into his head and commanded him to, "Stop that."

Defutois looked to the skinny man sitting beside Maupertuis and his eyebrows quizzed Quantz.

"That is the renowned, if not infamous Julien Offray de la Mettrie."

"I thought he was dead," Defutois responded.

"Wishful thinking" Quantz quipped. "Frederick gave him refuge when the Catholic Church kicked him out of France."

Defutois looked closer at the man's neck extended in raucous laughter and saw the malicious gleam in his eyes.

"It seems," Quantz continued, "that the Jesuits did not take kindly to de la Mettrie claiming that there is no such thing as a soul."

Defutois nodded his enlightenment and remembered the rage de la Mettrie's theories had ignited. Just a few years before, church and state in France had united to condemn de la Mettrie's thesis that man was merely a machine. Bishops, fearing the loss of their incomes and kings mindful of the loss of their heads, had excommunicated the heretic who dared to say that absolute monarchs and infallible popes were nothing more than noisy apes dressed in expensive robes.

"Being French," Quantz added, "others say the treason in his philosophy was that the human being is merely a creature who eats. He believes that man is nothing more than a digestive system. A long tube where we ingest nourishment, extract sustenance, and expel waste. Rather like a very complicated, and occasionally sentient, slug."

Quantz chortled to Defutois. "I have read his discourses and conclude that de la Mettrie's vocal cords are situated at the end of the tube farthest from his teeth."

Defutois laughter was brought to an abrupt end by the audience rising at the entrance of the King. Defutois started to clap, but Quantz quickly grabbed his hands. "Germans applaud only after the performance."

Frederick entered the salon with a middle-aged, portly man dressed in a French coat of the finest thread. Frederick laughed at some bon mot whispered beneath the screeching of chairs pushed back by the rising throng. He stood before the assembly and spread his hand to their guest.

"Noted Academicians of the Prussian Academy, Gentlemen of Discernment and Taste, Faithful Servants, and Trusted Friends. We are met here in this place to pay homage to genius. Monsieur Jacques de Vaucanson has travelled the considerable distance and inconvenient journey from Lyons to share with us the fruits of his knowledge of mechanics. We are especially blessed that he has brought with him two examples of the practical applications of his theoretical innovations which will be of benefit to us all."

Frederick stepped to the side to allow all eyes and ears to focus on the man standing between them and the tables behind him. Vaucanson bowed deeply to the departing monarch, as Frederick sat in his chair between de la Mettrie and Maupertuis, who thrilled at his presence.

"Gentlemen and Loyal Servants of His Majesty, to be invited to speak with you is an honor I may not survive, for the rest of my life will be only the denouement to this moment. We are all agreed that mathematics and science have vanquished superstition. I bring to you this day the first-born of the new thinking."

Vaucanson nodded to his assistant waiting vigilantly for the command and the nod that would send him into motion. With the slightest raising of Vaucanson's eyebrow, the assistant gently pulled the sheet away from the table and slowly revealed a woman sitting with a flute to her mouth.

The salon leaned forward to inspect the lady demurely displayed before them but were at a loss to understand what was before their very eyes. Quantz wanted to stand on a chair to get a better view but nothing could induce him to adopt such an undignified stance. He shaded his eyes to peer at the two hands holding a flute perpendicular to the lips. Defutois could not restrain his curiosity and asked, "What is that?"

"It purports to be some kind of musician," Quantz replied.

"Is it alive?" Defutois speculated.

Stephan was quick to explain, "It claims to be alive."

"What's she doing?" joined in Heinz.

The quartet of servants separated by the window sill were as mystified by the scene as everybody else in the salon. Heinz rested an elbow on the sill and placed his head so that he could see everything that was happening and draw no attention to himself. Stephan stood with his arms folded over his chest, as if waiting for a suicide to fall from a high steeple. Quantz' fingers stroked his chin but his face could not conceal from Stephan the look of vague apprehension coupled with the weary dismissal of something unworthy of his attention. He became more animated, when he saw Vaucanson nod to the assistant.

The young man dropped the sheet to the floor and touched something at the back of the table. The woman lifted her head.

The room gasped at this simple motion, but when she raised the flute to her lips, astonished silence erupted in their midst. Every body was inclined to the statue. Every ear was opened and all eyes bore into the cloud of expectation Vaucanson had released.

They saw her bosom swell and her lips purse to play a single note. The sound was as quiet as distant thunder promising more as it approached. She pressed the three fingers of her left hand to cover three holes on the flute and sounded a different note. They were captivated when she lifted the fourth finger of her right hand. The note jumped one step of the scale. Her finger thumped the flute and the sound crashed back to the first note.

Vaucanson stood taller in triumph and proclaimed, "I give you The Shepherdess." He bowed to the performer and gracefully backed away, leaving one hand extended in invitation to and commendation of the woman.

As if to bid him adieu, the Shepherdess continued to play the two notes. Her index finger increased the tempo into a lively trill on the notes but then ceased abruptly.

Quantz felt his face flush and his wig become moist. The trill was extended until the pitch of the notes was butchered by the movement of her fingers. He wanted to thrash the girl for making such a simple mistake on two easy notes, but quickly pressed his feet onto the floor and clenched his jaws.

Defutois stood with his mouth agape and mind rushing with questions. He turned to see Stephan's face glowering over the window sill and Heinz' arms forming a tripod for his bored chin. Heinz slouched up to the edge of the window, looked down at the orange trees, and picked his nose.

Frederick was in a fit of delight and marched up to the Shepherdess to stare into her face. She slowly blinked and the coquettish gleam of her eyes forced Frederick to withdraw two paces. Her pose offered delights he neither would nor could requite. His repulsion at her person turned to amazement when she dropped in sequence the middle and ring fingers of her right hand. The movement of the sounds was as precise as the marching of his guards.

She breathed again, snapped back all of her fingers and set them down to cover all the holes of the flute. Frederick's intrigue drew his face as close to the Shepherdess' mouth as he could dare. The fingers flared in sequence for her to produce part of a scale. Frederick's eyes wobbled along the flute, trying to follow the warbling of her notes. He paced around her, as if searching for the sources of the sound.

The audience could not contain itself and stood to huddle closer to the mystery. Defutois breathed in the excitement of the salon, but the silence was complete. No overturned chair crashed to the floor in the rush of academicians to the front.

They jostled each other like peasants around a dancing bear. All ears were on the Shepherdess and all eyes on the King.

Her chest billowed and she played a slow melody of five notes. The court was enthralled by her pastoral lullaby and could easily imagine her soothing the sheep on some sylvan pasture. The tune drove Frederick and the court back to the safety of their seats.

Vaucanson stood before his wonder, his eyes casting subtle instructions to his assistant. The helper thrust his arm behind the statue and waited for her to finish her song. At the very end, he allowed her note to linger, until he pressed a hidden lever and brought her performance to an abrupt end.

Quantz stood with his back to the wall. As the room erupted into applause, he bowed to ask Defutois, "What do you think of this exhibition?"

"I have never heard such a wonder."

"Let us hope we do not have to hear it again."

Quantz' desire was quickly quashed when Vaucanson stepped forward, bowed graciously to the court, and deeper to the King, but did not forget to stretch forth an admiring arm to the Shepherdess.

The court rose and Frederick led their ovation to the miracle they had witnessed. Frederick gazed avariciously at the statue, but Quantz recognized that frown of disappointment. He turned to Vaucanson and his hands commended the inventor to the court. "Please, Monsieur, initiate us into the mysteries of this marvel."

Vaucanson beamed a victorious smirk with a hint of viciousness to his captives and waited for their complete attention. His voice crept through the silence.

"My Comrades of the New Age, it is as much an honor as it is a joy to share with such distinguished minds the products of invention. You have witnessed and heard the future."

Vaucanson sensed the anticipation in the room and allowed it to simmer until his audience was about to burst in curiosity. His speech mixed fact with fascination and teased questions and desire in their nodding heads.

"Gentlemen. Men of discerning intellect and unquestionable authority. She has no mind. She has no morals. Her only pleasure is her function, to delight us with her music. The Shepherdess is the perfect woman."

Frederick's laughter rang through the hall, supported by the courtiers' agreeable guffaws and peals of extravagant chortles.

"Because she is completely lacking in any moral code, she can never be conflicted in the mind she does not possess."

Quantz saw de la Mettrie's head vehemently nod his assent to Vaucanson's statement. Quantz also wondered if he could make the same sounds as the Shepardess if he blew into de la Mettrie's ear and used his skull as a conch shell. He concluded that he could get a clearer tone out of a philosopher's empty head than from this posturing machine pretending to be a musician.

Vaucanson knew the moment to conclude his thesis. "Therefore, she can never do wrong because it is impossible for her to distinguish between right and wrong. She cannot think. She can only act. She is completely function without thought. The perfect peasant, eternally waiting for that higher power which will free her from inertia and set her in motion."

He raised an arm and the assistant pulled a lever at the back of the statue. The Shepherdess commenced a lively peasant dance that had them all nodding in time and tapping their feet. Her fingers rose and fell to produce a tune as boisterous as it was loud, but Quantz could hear the clicking of her fingers at each note.

Frederick swayed with the rustic rhythm and the court took this as permission to clap in time to the lady's performance. Quantz knew the tune, recalled from a distant childhood. He was so familiar with the melody that his ear could navigate the thumping of pulpy hands to hear the old tune being butchered.

He looked over their heads to watch the motions of her chest. He started to count the rises and falls of her bosom and quickly realized that there was no connection to the movements of her fingers. There was no breath. The chest moved in its own cycle, separate from the hand. The breathing was just a trick to produce the illusion of playing music.

Quantz closed his eyes to concentrate on the notes. Yes, there was sound, but there was also the ugliness of the unthinking performer. Each note was slightly out of tune. He heard the fumbling between notes that betrayed the incompetence of the self-assured player. He could have easily fixed such a simple problem. The slightest variation on the airstream over the mouthpiece would immediately turn this jumble of bleats into music. A few days of concentrated practice would rid the player of these annoying and sloppy habits. But that would be impossible. This thing could not improve with practice. It could only repeat. The clicking of her finger joints rattled in his ears and he said to himself. "This student needs a good oiling."

That was when it all became perfectly clear. The air was not coming from the mouth. There was some mechanism to feed the air directly into the flute. All the finger movements were just changing the flow of the air, but that flow was constant. That was why each note slurred into the next. That was why there was such a boring slide through the whole melody. Where the human could make distinct sounds that moved from one to the other like pearls of delicate and different hues on a string, this monstrosity could only smear sounds over one's ears. The rest of the Sheperdess' movements were all dedicated to creating the illusion of a woman playing a flute. What he was actually hearing was a bagpipe dressed in a peasant's frock. This marvel of the age was a fraud.

The audience sensed Vaucanson's hesitation and waited eagerly for him to cast yet more pearls. Frederick sat between his distinguished guest and his collection of geniuses sharing their impatience. He leaned forward when Vaucanson raised his chin.

"Esteemed Gentlemen, Royal Defender of Reason, my pleasure this day is exceeded only by my hope that you will appreciate the more immediate and practical benefits of the wonders only suggested by the Shepherdess's music. She entertains us with her talent but she also enlightens us with her methods of delight."

Vaucanson saw Frederick's face merge into equal proportions of curiosity and annoyance, so he skipped his preamble and cut to the heart of the matter.

"There is vast prosperity in war."

Vaucanson knew he had caught the King. Quantz had to stretch his neck to winnow every word over the heads of the court.

"Imagine industry and agriculture creating their products with the same efficiency as the Shepherdess creates her music. Think of her not as a simpleton, but as an incarnation of the concept of the machine in the service of man. Imagine the swaying of wheat in a field waiting to be reaped. Where it would take one hundred peasants a week to harvest a crop, a variation on the Shepherdess could accomplish the same task in a day. Such a machine would require the labor of only ten men."

The economics of the implication were instantly clear to everybody in the room. Vaucanson paused to let the idea settle and when he knew the seed was planted, watered it with more of what they wanted.

"Whole nations could feed on the fecund harvests gathered by such a machine. Hunger would be vanquished and famine would no longer consume His Majesty's subjects."

Frederick liked the idea of a machine making him the savior of his people and was eager for more of Vaucanson's economics.

"What, you ask, is to become of the rest of the peasants?" Vaucanson queried. "If ten men can bring in a harvest, will the ninety remain idle? We all know that he who does not work will not eat. Therefore, simple morals demand that we supply those ninety idle hands with the means to labor for themselves and their families."

Frederick nodded his assent and the court bubbled with the implications of the fact of idle hands making the devil's work.

"If we do not give relief to those whose work is made superfluous by the mechanization of their tasks, they will quickly become dissatisfied and revolt. In the hands of the hungry, pitchforks soon become weapons."

The court grew silent at this hint of revolution, and Frederick looked at the Shepherdess as if she were a threat.

"I say we exchange those pitchforks for muskets." The court was aghast at this last statement. Vaucanson had conjured the idea of rebellion and now he seemed to be advocating armed revolution.

"Look at this as if you were an idle farmhand. Faced with the possibility of starvation, you will grasp at any relief. The surest and quickest way to replace the sustenance lost from useless labor is to don Prussian blue and serve in His Majesty's armies."

Quantz saw that Frederick breathed deeply. It was the same sigh he had heard many times when Frederick had successfully learned a new way of tonguing the music he was attempting to wrestle from the instrument. The mention of uniforms was always a relief to The Soldier King.

"Indeed, one such harvesting machine would not only yield a cornucopia of crops, it would also swell the ranks of the royal service."

The courtiers turned automatically to one another and nodded furiously in agreement with this latest prophecy of science with the promise of sure and certain prosperity.

"It is a matter of simple arithmetic." One field of rye produces enough bread to fill five hundred bellies and creates ninety soldiers. Imagine five thousand such fields. The final account would be an additional four hundred and fifty-thousand soldiers. This is truly a march of progress."

Stephan's folded arms were so tight, he felt that he was being choked by a snake. He released his grip upon himself and sucked in enough air to dissipate his rage. He knew perfectly well what would happen to those ninety useless mouths, once they donned the mantles of infantry blue.

"Whoever controls such force will create an empire greater than Rome. The majesty of such a state will make Alexander look like a village bully."

Quantz could only admire Vaucanson's strange ability to say exactly what Frederick wanted to hear. It was as if the Frenchman was acting from a playbook written by some intimate of the King.

"The invincibility of this army will have costs to the bodies of the troops. War means fighting and fighting means killing. So it has always been, but the victor receives the spoils. The profits of this enterprise will be so much greater than the blood expended."

Vaucanson's audience was stunned into silence. Quantz thought of the cost of "this enterprise" and knew there was no antidote to the poison released into Frederick's ear. The combination of a larger purse and an immense army was an alchemy Frederick had been seeking for as long as he had been ruler. Vaucanson was offering him the possibility of turning the base metal of his people into gold.

"The blood sacrificed on the fields of glory will feed Mother Earth. Mars will make Demeter fertile and the crop yield will be great. Your Majesty's enemies will grow excellent potatoes."

Frederick howled and the audience followed his lead. Vaucanson smiled at the uproar of his last statement and waited delicately for the laughter to subside.

Vaucanson stood to the side, so that the audience would get a better view of his protege. Frederick looked around to examine his expectant court, but quickly snapped his face to the front when he heard the notes.

The Shepherdess launched into a performance and from the first sounds, everybody recognized The King's March. The tune that hovered over Potsdam like confetti at a wedding was taken up by the courtiers. Frederick sat beaming to hear his own composition become an anthem to his nobility led by such a talented machine.

Quantz remained silent, but quickly interrupted Defutois joining the chorus. "If you sing, they will all know you have learned German." Defutois snapped his mouth shut, but was reassured when Quantz told him, "Now you can applaud like a good German." Defutois banged his palms in time to the march and silently spied all the happy singers shouting the song with such gusto.

Frederick sat bemused at this display of loyalty from his court and his servants. There was a rare thrill in the graciousness of Vaucanson teaching the Shepherdess to play his tune. He savored every moment to the very end, and when the Shepherdess' chin dropped with the last note, he bowed to her with sincere affection.

He recalled Vaucanson to the centre of the salon, through the hubbub of the audience, and told him to continue with more of his marvels. Vaucanson's bow was the signal for silence, so the court waited for whatever would be his next astounding gift.

"We have witnessed the marvels of mechanics with our own eyes and ears. I have merely presented you with possibilities potent within the science of our little flute player. But now, Gentlemen, we must move from the sublime to the ridiculous, for we discover the thought that is laudable only in the act that is laughable."

He moved to the second table which was also hidden under a drape and the assistant stood at attention, waiting for Vauncanson's order to reveal whatever was nestling below the sheet. Vaucanson's hands beckoned the audience's attention and their presence. "Come closer, for this next wonder is somewhat smaller than the first."

The court rushed forward to crowd around the table in titillated expectation and Frederick joined the throng of gazers. Vaucanson nodded to the assistant and the sheet was whipped away to reveal a duck.

Frederick was the first to lean his hands upon the table and peer at the animal resting on what looked like pond water. "What is it?" he demanded. Vaucanson smiled over the royal pate and proudly exclaimed. "As the machine has conquered the goddess of music, so too can we now demand that nature obey our commands." He nodded to the assistant, who fiddled with a lever.

The duck immediately spread its wings and shook the water from its head. The closest courtiers were delighted to be deluged by the little creature and twittered their approval of the thing. The assistant pulled the lever again and the duck waggled its beak and lowered its head into the water. It shook its wings again and rose to present Frederick with a fish. Frederick politely refused the offering and the duck seemed to shrug its shoulders before swallowing the fish.

The courtiers marveled at the display of feeding and Belfort even exclaimed, "Look. You can see the fish going down the creature's throat." Frederick's attention was taken from Belfort to the gullet of the thing. "Yes. Look. It is eating the fish."

Vaucanson smirked his assent and explained, "Not just feeding but the whole process of digestion is evident in the creature's behavior." He looked at Frederick and challenged, "Your Majesty can prove this by placing your hand behind the duck."

Frederick's eyes narrowed with the possibility of some fun, so he told Belfort. "This is a function for our Baron of the Chancery. Belfort, lend us a hand."

The Baron was eager to please at any cost to himself and obeyed. The assistant twiddled with the lever, the duck waggled its tail, and filled Belfort's waiting palm with a mound of digested fish. The court roared with laughter even as the air became fetid. Belfort laughed the heartiest and offered his putrid prize to all around him. He held the ordure with all the reverence of a communion wafer and all the pride of receiving a medal from the king. In their mirth, the courtiers refused his gift, so Belfort stood holding the moist stool and slightly perplexed in his gratitude for all their attentions.

Quantz stood at the back of this display, utterly appalled at the scene. His face shone with the revulsion he felt.

Stephan nudged his shoulder and said, "You could make a fortune, if you bred the Shepherdess with the duck."

"And create yet another monstrosity?"

"A very profitable monster. Every court would purchase such a toy, if you could make her burp in French and the duck fart in German.

Chapter 7

Reconnaissance

Quantz nursed his vexation in a cloud of Stephan's pipe smoke. Anna did not complain about Stephan's tobacco because she knew it helped him think. She could always open the windows and light a candle to evict the noxious stink. For now, she would serve them coffee huddled around the table and let them work through their problems without nagging. Keeping a halter on Heinz was a greater challenge.

"If only we could examine that infernal device," Stephan blew a cloud of frustration over the table.

"There has to be some trick to it," Defutois added.

"Of course there is a trick," Quantz agreed, "and a very cunning one."

"In France, I heard much talk about Vaucanson's schemes," Defutois confessed.

"You know this man?" Quantz asked suspiciously.

"I know of his products, and if they are the measure of the man, then the man is as contrived as his inventions."

"He came to Dresden," Stephan contributed, "but I never saw his machines."

"I wonder what Duke Augustus thought of him?" Quantz mused.

"Augustus was not enthusiastic. He claimed that he had no need of mechanical bastards because he made enough of his own."

"So, Vaucanson found no wealthy patron in Dresden?" Quantz surmised.

"He was chased out of Lyons," Defutois affirmed.

"A crime?" Quantz asked.

"The worst."

"Seduced a nun?" Anna asked.

"Ruined the city." Defutois continued.

"An arsonist?" Stephan queried.

"Vaucanson is shrewd," Defutois said, "He and everybody with common sense could see that the entire population depended on lace and cloth for trade and for profit."

"This is not news," Stephan protested.

"But what he did is news," Defutois added.

They all leaned in to hear better.

"He invented a machine that could produce lace. The lace was perfectly uniform, without a knot or a blemish. Once the machine was set up and fed with hundreds of spindles of silk thread, it would knit twenty yards of lace in two hours. It would take fifty lace makers a week to compete with the machine."

"That is just like his lecture, praising the benefits of a machine to bring in the harvest," Quantz recalled.

"Would not that be a very good thing?" Anna asked.

"For a short time, yes," Defutois explained, "but the more lace it produced, the lower the price of the product. After a month, the profits of the mill owners were so reduced as to impoverish the richest men in Lyons."

"So, his machine put the owners out of business." Stephan said.

"Not only that. The machine replaced the lace workers. Without the work, there was such a threat of starvation that even the bakers wanted Vaucanson's head on a pole because nobody could afford their bread. A disaster."

"That's why he left Lyons?"

"Leave?" Defutois chuckled. "He thrashed his horses just to keep a few steps ahead of the mob. They had to be satisfied with burning his effigy in the city square because Vaucanson, the man, had escaped their clutches. The city fathers were happy to warm their hands at that pyre because they couldn't reach Vaucanson's neck."

"What happened to the machine?"

"The lace makers took off their wooden shoes and threw them at the machine until it became useless, but they gave us a new word for the French language."

"What is that?" Quantz asked.

"A wooden shoe is a 'sabot' so destroying the machinery became 'sabotage.' I am happy to say that the tradition has been exported to other cities of my country with even greater success."

"Why should this please you?" Stephan prodded.

"Think of the consequences which Vaucanson made so explicit in his talk. All the men made unemployable by his machine would produce an inexhaustible supply of cannon fodder for the wars."

"I found that peculiarly distressing," Quantz confessed.

"The final product of this machine is poverty and murder on a scale we cannot imagine," Defutois concluded.

They sat perplexed, staring into the dregs of coffee. Anna knew her husband was very upset by this king's toy, but would not intrude upon his brooding. When he really needed her advice, she would willingly help as much as she could. Until then, she would hold her tongue. She calmly refilled their cups.

Quantz raised his cup and their curiosity when he said, "All the more reason to discover how it works."

"We can't get into the salon," Stephan observed.

"The guards lock it," Defutois remembered.

"I have the key to the music chamber," Quantz said with an air of eager conspiracy.

"The music room does not connect with the salon," Stephan explained. "The salon is an island reserved for His Majesty's most honored guests."

"If we could only find a way to that island," Quantz grumbled.

They sat disappointed in their plans. Quantz was enjoying their plotting of the elaborate, schoolboy prank but saddened with the realization that their scheme was doomed to failure before it even began.

Anna decided that it was time to get them on their quest. "What you need is a guide," she pronounced. The simple truth was so obvious it embarrassed them that they had not thought of it.

"Where would we find such a person to usher us into the royal presence when it is elsewhere?"

"In the kitchen," Anna said as she disappeared from the dining room.

"What is she talking about?" Stephan whispered to Quantz.

"We are about to find out," Quantz laughed, "and be prepared for my wife to produce the perfect solution to our problem."

Anna entered with Heinz beaming at her side

"I can," said Heinz.

"The door to the salon is locked," Stephan challenged.

"I can still get in. I've done it many times."

"Why do you do that?" Quantz

"Just to see." Heinz said with pride.

Anna knew she had challenged them, but wanted to be useful to their schemes. She also appreciated the danger of court servants, no matter how favored, being caught skulking around the palace where they were not needed. She had given them Heinz, not only to help them, but also to protect them.

"It is too great a risk," Stephan admitted.

"Not now," Heinz assured them.

"Why now?" Quantz asked.

"Because Grigori is on guard duty."

"This Grigori will just let us in?" Stephan asked.

"No. Grigori is one of the Giants."

"What is a giant?" Defutois asked.

They all erupted into laughter, until Quantz explained. "There is a Prussian tradition of collecting the tallest men for the first regiment of the King's Guard."

"They are all huge," Anna shared. "They are two meters tall and they wear high hats with a big golden badge at the front."

"To be a Giant of the Guard is a high honor," Quantz explained. "Their families get triple the guardsman's pay, just because they have bred a son who stands head, shoulders, and chest above all their other children."

Heinz laughed louder than all the rest, until Anna slapped him on the shoulder. "Giants are just like everybody else, only they are very big," he said. "Grigori is the stupid one. He will march around the palace with his musket to his shoulder and his belt making noises like a cow bell."

"But he is the guard," Defutois complained.

"He will walk for two hours and not look to the left or to the right," Heinz explained.

"So we enter the salon when he is not marching?" Defutois said

"When he turns the corner, I will let you in," Heinz said.

"You know how to do this?"

"Of course."

"If the palace was on fire, Grigori would march straight through the flames, never wondering why his wig was burning."

Heinz' confidence shamed them all into action.

Anna scolded them about talking too much and doing too little. Heinz was like a horse held by Anna's apron reins and was clearly itching for an adventure. "If you are going to do this, it must be now. Finish it while there is still daylight left," she proclaimed.

Quantz seemed to have been waiting for Anna's orders. He rose from his chair and stated the obvious. "We'll be no wiser sitting here." He turned to Heinz and bowed in submission. "Lead on, my little scout."

Heinz' chest swelled with the pride of the truly useful, but he commanded them, "You go to the door and I'll open it."

With that instruction, he was out the door and disappeared into the twilight.

"You heard him," Anna insisted, and the men trooped after the child. Anna bade them adieu and told them there would be sweets waiting upon their return.

Quantz led the them through the streets toward the palace. The last of the day seemed to hug the tree branches over their heads. The baker cast his greeting as he shuttered his windows and the blacksmith's forge was settling into a dull rest. They were soon free of the throngs of Potsdam's late afternoon shoppers.

Defutois felt like a naughty schoolboy carried along by his braver companions, so the serious scowl on Quantz' face did not infect him with cowardice. Stephan was used to being on the wrong side of a tradesman's curfew and was eager to get to his quarry. Quantz knew he could talk himself out of being discovered in the palace and was confident in his alibi of collecting music for His Majesty in case of discovery. They mastered their trepidation as they approached the steps to the terrace. Twilight would be no impediment to their quest.

Halfway up the curving stairway, Stephan's tongue clicked in admonition when Quantz' shoes scuffed a stone step and the three stood rigid at an approaching sound.

Rhythmic, iron-shod footsteps rang from the side of the building and they all stood rigid at the echo. They kept low on the stairs so that the topmost step hid their heads. Just as Heinz had informed them, Grigori marched around the corner and passed them along the terrace, looking straight ahead. They waited until the regular thumping of Grigori's heels faded around the far corner and stealthily snuck to the salon door.

Quantz felt foolish, waiting for he knew not what. Stephan examined the woodwork of the frame, but Defutois stood back to cast wary glances along the terrace, fearful that the giant would return. A curtain swung back and Heinz' victorious face grinned assurances to them through the window pane. He disappeared and they heard a click. The door opened a crack, and Heinz ushered them into the King's most public chamber.

They stood before the draped figures, quiet as waiting corpses. Quantz commanded, "The Shepherdess" and Heinz pulled the drape and mischievously disrobed the lady. She sat serene in her casual defiance and Quantz felt hate rush through his body. He told himself that this was just a thing and there was nothing to fear from her, but there was also the suspicion that this was an extremely dangerous foe.

Stephan examined the base of the woman's plinth and his fingers soon discovered four carved roses at the corners of a panel. They moved slightly to his touch and he quickly realized that the foliage was more functional than decorative. The rose buds cunningly concealed the screws which held the panel in place. He turned one flower to the left and released the corner with a slight spring. He nodded to Defutois. "Hold your hands close to the bottom in case it falls." Defutois squatted on command and caressed the base of the plinth with the heels of his hands. Stephan held both petaled keys between his firm thumb and fingers and gently twisted the left rose. Defutois caught the freed panel and held it until Stephan placed it on the floor so that it would not crash.

The night was fast approaching, but there was just enough light for them to peer under the table and into the mechanism. Quantz immediately realized that he could not fathom the tangle of wires, rods, and tubes which commanded the Shepherdess's performance. Defutois could not contain his amazement, "Good God. What is that?" Stephan allowed the silence to seep into Defutois' curiosity before telling him, "It is nothing more than a collection of gears and pulleys cunningly contrived to produce an illusion."

Quantz could see delicate metal teeth touching what looked like a net. "How has he created the sound?" he demanded with irritated curiosity. Stephan's finger prodded the net and they could see the teeth of the many gears cunningly fitted into the holes in the net. "This scroll engages the gears and the gears control the rods that move the fingers." Stephan pressed on a rod and a finger on the figure jumped from the hole of the flute. There was a slight sighing no louder than a baby's kiss as air escaped, but they all jumped back as if from sudden thunder.

Heinz had been examining the front of the figure and lifted the Shepherdess's skirt. "She has no legs," he exclaimed in wonder. They giggled as silently as they could, suppressing their amusement with fist stoppered lips until Stephan whispered, "She doesn't need legs. She's not that type of courtesan."

When they had regained enough composure to continue their examination, Quantz asked, "But the breath?" They watched Stephan's fingers move over the net and twist around a rod until they rested beside a canvas bag. Stephan smiled the grin of the truly initiated, "It's a simple bladder." He pressed the bag and one note sounded from the flute. He sat back on his haunches and exclaimed in grudging admiration, "He's waxed a simple canvas bag."

"Why?" Quantz demanded.

"So the air will not escape on its way to the figure's mouth."

Quantz nodded in assent but shrugged to repeat the query. "Of course, all the air has to go through the mouth, but how does it get there?"

Stephan pinched a purple tube and could feel the pressure of the air it contained respond to his touch. "It's a tube. Some pliable material, but stronger than the air it contains."

Defutois watched in wonder as Quantz delicately ran his fingers up the tube from the bladder. He lifted the back of the figure's dress with his free hand and could see the tube he grasped snake into her head. He released the tube and felt safe when he heard the mechanism hiss.

He stepped silently around the table and plinth to stand with Heinz gazing into the face. They could hear Stephan's heavy breathing and his hands making little rattling noises in the statue's head. They heard his demand, "See what happens now." They stood waiting and heard a metallic screech beneath Stephan's probing fingers.

One note from the flute filled the salon, and Quantz instinctively pulled the flute away from the thing's mouth. In the liberating silence, they heard the stream of air spray through the mouth and miss the flute. Quantz waited for the hissing to stop and released the hands that held the instrument. The Shepherdess' arms retracted to their original position. Heinz looked as if he had seen a ghost, but his ears were more attuned to the more distant crunching. "Back" he commanded.

Quantz, Stephan, and Defutois immediately sprang to the columns between the windows and listened to their own heartbeats. Grigori's steps drew nearer, but his pace remained as constant as the Shepherdess' fingers. Quantz noticed Heinz was breathing in time to Grigori's marching feet. Stephan's back hugged the column and his eyes, filled with resolve to surrender to whatever would happen, stared straight ahead. Defutois crouched and restrained his head from popping up to see.

Grigori's predestined sentry route led him further along the terrace, and his receding footsteps breathed relief into the salon. Heinz' finger bid the giant adieu and his voice echoed the confidence of his many forays into the forbidden reaches of the palace. "He's gone."

They gathered at the Shepherdess' rump, bent over with their hands upon their knees and examined her metal entrails. They peered at the cogs and wheels, desperate that their augury would give them understanding. Quantz was mystified by the rods connecting her fingers to the mechanism, but was determined to purloin knowledge from their act of defiant intrusion. He turned a questioning gaze upon Stephan.

"This thing is just a very big clock that can pump air."

"What about the music?" Defutois asked.

"It's just sound," Quantz assured him. "Music is what you do with the sound."

"So it isn't music at all."

"It just imitates music," Quantz pronounced.

Stephan pointed to the bladder and exclaimed, "The air comes from here. It is generated by this clockwork pressing and releasing a set of bellows. Quantz saw the collapsed edges of the bellows and was intrigued when Stephan expanded them. "Listen," Stephan ordered. He gently pressed the canvas triangle and the flute sounded above their heads. Quantz grinned the smile of the newly initiated. The Shepherdess held no more mysteries for him.

"So," he said to Stephan, "this is a more elaborate version of a cuckoo-clock."

"Exactly," Stephan assured him. "Those Swiss contraptions are all the rage, but they sing the same song every hour. I am sure they both disappoint and bore the birds who hear them."

Defutois' admiration for Vaucanson's genius immediately dissipated. Their excursion into the bowels of the player proved they were dupes. "This is no better than some gypsy fortune-teller assuring you of what you most desire."

"Well said, Frenchman," Quantz exclaimed. "And this thing is just as false as those predictions."

Defutois suddenly realized that his education was sadly deficient. When he had heard the Shepherdess perform that afternoon, he had been amazed. Now he knew that his wonderment was at the mechanical and that the mechanism was not the music.

Stephan still appreciated the sheer genius of the invention, but he was disgusted by such talent wasted on a mere toy. Quantz concluded their thoughts when he proclaimed, "There's more music in a hunting horn and a pack of dogs than in this."

Heinz had lost interest in the lady's skirts, but his ear was tuned to the terrace. He heard the distant crunch of gravel and dim voices. Heinz risked discovery, but had to peep through the window. He saw Baron Belfort and de la Metrie standing on the terrace at the stop of the stairs and arguing. Quantz heard the insistent tones through the window and froze before the statue. Heinz heard two more steps crunch towards them and commanded, "Let's go."

Stephan and Defutois quickly replaced the mannequin's back panel and together cast the sheet over the Shepherdess. It was with some relief that Quantz took his position behind Heinz, standing at the door to the palace's corridors. He listened to Belfort and de la Metrie hammering each other in wrangling discourse. They were so engaged in their verbal fencing that they ignored the salon's windows. Quantz sighed in relief as they carried their debate along the terrace. Stephan and Defutois formed a line behind Quantz and realized that they were to follow Heinz through the palace to make their escape.

When he opened the door to listen to a distant chattering, Heinz knew his way was safe and guided his charges out of the salon and along the corridor to a flight of steps. Quantz had never seen these stairs because he had no reason to use them. They silently but assuredly placed their feet where Heinz' shoes had been and felt they were in some steamier part of the building. "This is the scullery," Heinz informed them as if they were on a tour. Heinz led them through mountains of clean pots that threatened to topple at their approach and clatter the alarm. They quickly entered a smaller hall and saw dusk swirling past an open door. Heinz stuck out his head to scan for danger and beckoned them onward. They entered a well-trodden path and crouched to follow their leader. Defutois smirked to think of himself on a warparty in a forest. "All I need is some facepaint to make me a handsome Iroquois," he chuckled to himself.

The aroma of horse dung and the clinking of harnesses confirmed that they were passing the stables. They skirted the windows releasing the ostlers' jovial complaining and scurried along the path to a smaller shed. Quantz heard someone hammering at a forge and felt a strange comfort in the memory of heated sweat dripping from a muscled chest.

Heinz, picked up their pace when they turned past the stables and into the lowest terrace of the palace. Amid the orange trees, pungent with acid juice, they stopped to regain their composure. The gates of the palace were just beneath them and Quantz was quick to praise Heinz. "You certainly know your way around," he complimented. Heinz thrilled to the praise and confessed, "I know all the places where there are no barons."

They sauntered casually through the gates, and Defutois felt an accomplishment that was entirely new to him. There was a pleasure in knowledge, no matter the risk they had run to acquire it. In the future, he would beguile guests with his adventure of the night, but he also knew it would be many, many years before he could relate the anecdote. Stephan kept close to Heinz, but his mind was sorting through the maze of mechanics and the jumble of gears he had seen. "Yes," he thought to himself, "it is a marvel, but to what purpose?"

Anna stood at the front door, happy to see the little procession wending its way along Potsdam's main street. She smiled to think they were alone, for if anything bad had happened, they would be accompanied by a palace guard.

Quantz was relieved to see Anna's smile. He stood proud before her when she asked, "So, you have been seeing another woman!"

Defutois was quick to respond, "Actually, we've been seeing right through another woman." They laughed at the quickness of his wit. Quantz recalled Defutois' story of the lacemakers of Lyons wrecking Vaucanson's devilish machines and exclaimed, "It makes me wish I wore wooden shoes."

The Memoir of Charles Defutois

Part the Third

Paris, Lazarette Prison,

July 26, 1794

I have become fascinated by the sunlight streaming through my window. If I am patient, it warms me. But as it heats, it speaks to me.

The light passes through the window's bars and forms a shadowy rectangle on the floor. The floor becomes a strange grid, a chessboard of quivering squares. But the day has its own bewildering shape.

At first light, the grid leans to the left. All the sections are twisted into files of increasingly acute triangles. Their lines are distinct but also vague, as if drawn with crumbling charcoal.

At the sun's zenith, the light is strong, mature, and the bars cast a rigid pattern upon the floor. The dark lines gouge themselves into a regularity that regiments the rectangles into a strict order.

With the setting of the sun, this proud formation begins to melt to the right, until twilight topples the twisted squares into evaporating night.

When I am patient, a memory forms in each of those cubes. They are like a display from a Magic Lantern but they move. The scenes are animate and I can watch in wonder the adventures of long ago, deeds that are more alive than any event trapped in pounded pigment and drying oil. The quadrangles become scenes from my life. Each part becomes a lucid picture of the whole, but there is only the merest suggestion of a thread connecting one to the other.

And now I loiter through each day's program, expectant for every caged narrative. Sometimes there is a picture, just a fog, an aroma conjured by a wisp of scent. Other times, the scene is a portrait so vivid that I must avert my gaze and try to blink it to oblivion. Such images are painted by knives; the colors bleed. They raise the ghosts but not the spirits. But the visitations wander from memory with the day. I must be as brave as Paul demands, and suffer through these apparitions.

I am intent to find out what happens next as each scene unfolds. I throttle the pictures to reveal a meaning I never knew when I was living through those twisted scenarios. I can become acquainted again with that youth in the coiffured wig and each day he is less a stranger. This is how I am making friends with myself.

Chapter 8

Silken Threads

Heinz lifted his elbow from the table to sniff his shirt. He loved the lingering fumes of the soap. Every week, Anna drowned the shirt in soapy water and attacked the collar with her brush. Then she turned the brush on the neck that produced the brown stains and ignored Heinz' protestations, "I'm clean enough." When the ordeal was over and the wind had almost dried the cloth, Anna thumped the wrinkles with the iron she kept ready on the stove. Heinz enjoyed the white pelt hissing under her firm hand. The sleeves billowed from his wrist buttons to his shoulder and the garment caressed his body with the warmth of a peasant's smock.

He brought his attention back to the parts of the flute scattered over the table and watched Quantz and Anna intently. Quantz held one tube firmly in his left hand and twisted some circular tool around the end of the tube. Quantz stopped to blow wood dust from the tube and inspect his handiwork. He was smoothing the ends into a recessed circular tongue, and Heinz blurted out his curiosity, "What does that do?"

Quantz showed him a flexible piece of metal that was smooth on one side and rough on the other. He wrapped the length of metal around the end of the tube and twisted slowly. To Heinz, it looked like Quantz was strangling the wood. "Does the tube become a plug?" he asked.

"What you call a plug is a tenon. The end of one tube must be smaller so it fits into the other tube," Quantz explained. Heinz nodded with as much understanding as mystification, but the process was becoming clearer as he watched Quantz work.

"It is the same way the legs are joined to this table and the chair on which you are sitting."

Anna smiled when she saw Heinz duck down to inspect the table legs. "There are little round things on the legs," he exclaimed with delighted amazement.

"A plug is to stop something, like a plug in a barrel to keep in the beer," Quantz added. "But the air must flow through the place where the two pieces meet."

Heinz nodded sagely and fingered the circle. Quantz was enjoying his lesson. "You can think of this part as a plug with a hole in it, but it is better to use the correct word, tenon, so people will know what you're talking about."

"So, this whole piece must have a tenon to connect with the hole," Heinz surmised.

"Exactly, but the hole is a socket."

Quantz offered the cylinder he held before Heinz' sparkling eyes. "This must have a tenon at both ends,"

"Because it must join two pieces," Heinz concluded.

Anna sat between them with her needle poised. "You are a quick learner, young man," and she patted his head.

"I agree," Quantz assured him, and Heinz relaxed into triumph.

Quantz pressed the metal ribbon tighter between his thumb and forefinger and gave the tube another twist. "A perfect circle cannot be made with a straight blade." Heinz' head dipped once to acknowledge the lesson. "It is better to cut the plug slowly with this pliant file." Quantz gave another twist to the tube, and Heinz watched tiny grains of wood speckle Quantz' fingers. "You can feel when the join is just right." Quantz slid the tube's tenon into the socket of the second section and stood it on its end.

Heinz leaned over the table to inspect the master's work and picked up the joined sections when Quantz told him, "Feel it for yourself." His inquisitive fingers grasped the tube, shook it, and heard a slight rattle. "They don't fit," he observed with some disappointment. Quantz laughed. "The join must be loose at this stage." He took back the two pieces and shook them beside Heinz' ear to make a delicate tremor. "My wife finishes the magic."

Heinz was now thoroughly confused, but he grasped the basic principle to marrying two tubes of wood together.

Anna smiled at them both and continued to pick the treads out of one of Quantz' lace cuffs. "You'll see how it's done," she assured Heinz. "Now, pay attention."

Her needle teased out a single thread of the lace. The more she pulled, the more the lace filagree became one long twisted line of silk. She grasped the end with her thumb and middle finger and pulled it to her elbow. When she was sure the line was as straight as she could get it, she took her scissors and snipped it at her elbow. She placed the line on the table, and Heinz said, "It looks like a very long worm."

She laughed and wondered to herself where he had seen such worms. Heinz watched her repeat the process, and a second line joined the first. Heinz saw that they were exactly the same length and waited for more.

"Now," she said, "we must make them perfectly straight." She threw one line into her mouth and pulled it through her teeth to remove the crinkles. The line was not to her liking, so she dragged it through her clenched jaws a second time. After casting an expert eye over the thread, she laid it on the table. Heinz stared long before saying, "It is perfectly straight."

"That is what is needed," she told him. "You try one," and she threw the second thread to her pupil. Heinz picked it up and followed Anna's example. He was a little too brutal with his teeth, so his thread sat beside Anna's looking like a flat ribbon.

"It has to be straight but also round," she criticized gently. Her fingers, elbow, and scissors flashed and she tossed another thread to Heinz. He pulled the thread through his teeth with less pressure and beamed when he compared it with Anna's work.

"It is very straight. A little too fat, but it will do," she said.

Quantz whispered to Heinz. "The thread must be just the right thickness and perfectly round."

"Why is that?" Heinz asked.

"You'll see," Quantz assured him.

Anna picked up an old candle end and drew the thread through the wax with her thumb and forefinger. Heinz's eyes carefully watched her slowly pull the thread straight. When she placed it on the table, the thread was almost rigid. Heinz feared to touch it, for the delicacy of Anna's fingers forbade him to interrupt her work.

She held one tube of the flute firmly in her left hand so that the tenon stood clear of her fingers. "Heinz, My Dear, we must wrap this thread very carefully around the tenon, so that when the flute is assembled, the tubes will be sealed and no air will escape through the joins."

She watched Heinz' face light up and explained, "All the parts must fit snugly together so they do not fall apart when the instrument is played."

Heinz focussed all of his curious attention on Anna's right hand as she pierced the end of the thread with her needle and skewered it to the base of the tenon. Her thumb clamped the thread and she withdrew her needle.

Heinz watched her fingers as if a village magician were conjuring sweets from thin air before his eyes. The needle picked up the other end of the thread and Anna bit it between her teeth. Her eyes widened to Heinz, telling him to pay attention. She pulled the thread tight between her teeth and the tenon. Her breath was hot on the thread and made the wax pliable. The needle in her right hand teased the thread around the tenon, as if she were winding a spool, until she was certain there was no overlap. Anna's needle pushed the end of the thread under the last turn of the coil. She pulled it tight and snipped off the excess.

Heinz felt the regularity of the raised binding. The tenon was now wrapped in little waxen ridges. He understood why the thread had to be pulled round, tight, and not flat. Now, the wax-wound, threaded tenons would hold the instrument together.

Quantz leaned back with his hands behind his head. There was something familiar in Heinz' concentration, but just what it was evaded his memory. When Heinz smiled his eager enthusiasm, Quantz noticed the left side of his grin was like tide-rotted posts at a deserted wharf. A trip to the barber was definitely necessary.

He watched Anna teach Heinz how to cut thread so it would not fray. The boy was able to make a passable joint in less than an hour and Quantz had to admit that Anna was an excellent teacher.

"This is new to you," she said with a hint of a question that Heinz avoided. "What do your parents do?"

"We have a farm and grow barley and pigs," he admitted, and Quantz heard the reluctant hesitation in his voice.

"Pigs are a lot of work," Anna prodded.

At the mention of pigs, Heinz' tongue was loosed from it reins. He waxed lyrical on the different kinds of animals and named some of his favorites. "Brutus is the biggest. He gave meat for a whole winter."

"I could not kill an animal with a name," Anna scowled.

"Brutus had a very good life. We used to play together and chase each other. When it was time, I held the Judas Bowl."

"What is that?" Quantz asked.

"You take a bowl with all the things a pig likes to eat and make a trail away from the others. Then you put down the bowl and when he is happy, you cut his throat."

Anna shuddered to think of Heinz slaughtering his playmate. Quantz saw the simple acceptance of the death in the boy's face. Peasants cannot afford to be sentimental if they do not wish to starve. But the calm relating of the end of Brutus made questions rise where Quantz did not really wish to find answers.

"Where is the farm?" Quantz asked.

"A little village near Dresden."

"Does this habitation have a name?"

"Yes. It's called Kaditz," Heinz admitted with great confidence.

Anna looked silently at Quantz whose eyes remained fixed on Heinz. Anna cast a critical eye over the table littered with plates, tools, and the dismembered flute. When he saw Heinz' eye glaze over with the fatigue of concentration, he nodded to Anna. "Right," she said, "enough for one evening. Off to sleep with you."

Heinz was quick to obey. He had learned that immediate submission was the key to all the fun Quantz offered, and the full stomach Anna provided. He rose and bowed to his patrons, who smiled and nodded, 'Good Night' before he scootled to the kitchen. Anna shouted after his retreating form, "Wash your face and hands."

She sat at the table, wondering how to speak of the things they both ignored. She cocked an ear to the sound of gurgling from a pail in the kitchen, and looked straight at Quantz.

He breathed a sigh, as if making a great effort to recall something he remembered so well. Anna was about to utter the name they dare not speak when Quantz simply said, "Kaditz."

She felt relief that he would acknowledge the place where he had courted a young widow and she had thrilled with the attentions of the Duke's master musician. She had not been able to bury her first husband. Whatever was left of him remained on some forgotten field where even a captain of artillery merited only a few shovels of earth. He had been a good man to her, even if his visits were rare and unexpected interruptions of his master's campaigns. The news of his death gave her neither shock nor regrets, only worry as to her future. A widow's pension was barely more than a pittance and there were no children to support her. The Captain was the past. Quantz offered a future with more promise than the bleak present.

Quantz picked up a tube, held it to his eye like a mariner's telescope, and framed Anna's face in the circle. He moved his eye-piece over her seated form and lingered at the full shoulders. He focussed his gaze on her fingers, blotched from years of dutiful, if complaining, scullery and sighed to think of all the work she did for him.

"What are you doing?" she queried.

"Trying to find out how many miles there are to Dresden."

He placed the tube on the table and Anna could not hide her blushes.

She remembered the mile-stone. Kaditz' only architectural diversion, indeed its only work of art, was an ornately carved stone signpost, leaning on its plinth and pointing the way to Dresden. Quantz' stare shrugged off the years between their table and the milestone, where they would rest on their walks before wending their way home. Kaditz was the farthest of their routes when they walked the country paths and grew accustomed to one another. The milestone was the place where Quantz had finally suggested that they marry. There was no great ceremony. No gift of rings or extravagant vows. There was just the admission of what they both feared to say, that "we should marry." It was not a supplication, "Will you marry me?" Neither was it some tentative suggestion that, "marriage is a very happy and honorable state." No. It was a straightforward proclamation of the very obvious fact of 'we'. This was something they would do together.

Anna had been delighted and a little confused. This Quantz sitting on the granite beside her was a sophisticated man of the world, but that world had not spoiled him. The other musicians and high servants were very aware of their dues from their masters and their rights over women. Quantz could defer to his master, even if he had no respect for him. But he was never more aloof to servants beneath his station than he was submissive to those above him. Anna had been impressed with the man's ability to perform his duties without using his station to hold power over others. Beneath the brocaded coat of the courtier, there was the dignity of the peasant. So, it was with the assurance that he was a good and decent man that she immediately said, "Yes," and they stood to walk back to Dresden and into their future together.

"It was ten kilometers," she recalled.

"You have a good memory."

"How can I forget?"

Their memories were invaded by the smacking of Heinz' lips from the kitchen. Anna turned a motherly ear to the door and Quantz watched her carefully. At the ruffle of a blanket, she rose and left the room. Quantz listened to the quiet creak of one floorboard under Anna's foot. She returned and sat before informing him, "He always throws off that blanket and is cold in the night."

"He also talks in his sleep," he added.

"What does he say?"

"Nothing very revealing. Sounds only he knows. Once he seemed to be having a dialogue with a horse collar, but I was unable to follow their conversation."

Quantz sensed her concern, but could not reassure her.

"He does not seem to know very much about Kaditz," he said.

"That is strange," she casually concluded.

They had been intrigued by Heinz' bucolic description of the family farm in Saxony. When he spoke of his sister cutting rows of barley in the fields, they became suspicious of his tale.

"There is no barley in Kaditz."

"There is hardly a farm to grow a crop."

"But it seems he is well acquainted with the slaughtering of pigs," Quantz surmised.

"You can raise swine anywhere."

"Or nowhere."

Anna fidgeted under the suspicions dredged up by their questions. She knew there were things that were better not said, even though she was bursting to know.

"Do you think the boy is a complete liar?" she finally asked.

"To create such an elaborate lie, the liar needs to know the truth," Quantz proclaimed.

"So he is not insane."

"It may be that such untruths are his only means of dealing with a truth too terrible to admit."

Quantz thought of the kindness Heinz offered when killing an animal he claimed was his playmate. He shuddered to think that the tale of the pig's demise hid an actual playmate. He had heard of children committing murders, but there was no proof that Heinz was one of that tribe. It could also be that there were no playmates. Brutus may have been his pet and only friend. He knew that they would never discover the truth from Heinz' lips. It was better to accept the lie, knowing that it was false, because the truth it hid should remain Heinz' secret.

The snoring from the kitchen crept into the dining room, and they turned their heads to the intrusion. Heinz' slow breathing assured Anna that he was sleeping comfortably, but the rhythm waltzed in Quantz' ears. He raised his arm and waved it in time to the snoring. "Poco Adagio," he commanded. Anna stifled a laugh to see her husband conducting the sleeping child. Quantz grinned in his humor until their attention was commanded by other noises over their heads.

They heard Stephan grumble his way out of the bed. Soon his feet tapped a trail across the upper room. The sliding of crockery was the overture to his performance on the chamber pot. Quantz smiled when the tinkling of Stephan's organ recital trickled through the floorboard. Quantz raised his arm and commanded the stream to flow "Andante," and listened for the renewal of Heinz' sleeping serenade.

Stephan's instrument merged into a smooth melody, so Quantz' arm led into "Ah, the legato."

His right hand drew in Heinz's nasal bass, with "Lento, Lento." The left hand was raised to the ceiling teasing, "Moderato" from the maestro. A rapid shake of Quantz' left hand, corresponded to the, "Presto" from above, and Anna stoppered her laughter with her fist.

His right hand kept Heinz at "Andante" but his other arm insisted that Stephan's recital become, "Prestissimo."

Anna begged him, "Stop. I'll wet myself."

Quantz cocked an ear to the ceiling and said, "Ah, the ritardando," and the cascade on high dwindled to a tired drip.

They heard Stephan grunt back to the bed and hugged each other to stifle their screams. Quantz cast a final wave to the kitchen for the finalé and "silencio" quashed Heinz' snores.

Anna broke their embrace to wipe her eyes and sighed, "What are we going to do with all our guests?"

Quantz took the hint and cheerfully confessed, "We are going to need a bigger house."

Chapter 9

Parquetry

Quantz mounted the last step to the terrace and the stillness stopped him. There was birdsong and wind soughing through the branches, but they were strangely subdued. His foot scraped the gravel at the next step but it felt like an intrusion. A few more steps brought him to the door of the music chamber and he stood looking through the window at Stephan's back bent over a table.

Stephan was sitting at a table sharpening a pencil. His thumb pushed a knife blade along the wood until the graphite became keener than a spearpoint. He was engaged in some study that demanded his whole attention, so Quantz was careful to turn the door handle very quietly. Even that little squeak sent Stephan flying out of his chair and the pencil soaring to the ceiling. He turned as if to confront a violent assailant and flew into a rage at Quantz. "What the Hell are you doing?"

Quantz attempted a supplicating and rare smile and begged forgiveness for breaking Stephan's concentration. "Breaking concentration?" Stephan shouted. "I almost filled my pants," he scolded. "Then I was about to break your head."

"I am so very fortunate that you have controlled both your desire to attack and your bowels," Quantz admitted. "Is it now safe to enter?" he asked.

Stephan sighed in resignation and motioned Quantz to join him. Whenever anyone took his attention from his work, he knew that it would be some minutes, indeed sometimes hours, before he could collect his mind and return to his task. He sometimes envied hermits, until he remembered that even monks with vows of silence had to be fed. "Well, you've ruined it for now. What are you doing here anyway?"

"I have to sort out the music. The king wants one copy for each of his residences. Since he is otherwise engaged, this is a good time to do it."

"That's why I'm here," Stephan said as his calm returned. "I have to do some measuring, when I am not being disturbed." Stephan spread his arm over the table as an invitation for Quantz to share his endeavors.

The table was a simple carpenter's bench, but it had hinged extensions at each end. Stephan had created the whole thing so it could be folded easily and quickly carried away when one of the masters needed the room immediately. Stephan had learned to vacate rooms efficiently, if his presence came between some nobleman and the immediate gratification of pleasure.

Quantz inspected the long roll of beige wallpaper Stephan had tacked to the table. Stephan's box of rulers, protractors, and pencils were strategically placed on the paper roll and Quantz' curiosity commanded his tongue.

"What are you doing with all this?"

"All this," Stephan stabbed his forefinger at the paper roll, "will become the floor."

Stephan pointed to the ceiling and Quantz saw a triangle of lead dangling from the center of the chandelier. "The whole room looks symmetrical, but that is an illusion," Stephan complained. Quantz looked again at the plumb line almost touching the floor and he thought it looked like a pendulum at rest.

Beneath the point of the line, Stephan had drawn chalk-lines from the center to the walls. Quantz studied the radiating lines and his eye followed them to the abrupt ends at the walls. The length of each line was different. Stephan threw up his hands in disgust when Quantz said, "A blind wheelwright could have created this wobbly circle."

"The problem will be that I must fit regular shapes to this disjointed monstrosity," Stephan grumbled.

He brought Quantz' attention back to the patchwork of rectangles, squares, and lozenges on the table. Indeed, Quantz thought, Stephan would have considerable difficulty transferring his design onto a floor. He had no doubt the finished product would be spectacular, but he was very curious as to how Stephan planned to make his idea a reality which would survive the feet endlessly tapping to the rhythms of an infinite line of notes.

"This will be considerably geometrical," Quantz mused.

"Yes. The straight lines under the feet will contrast with the twisted lines of the walls."

They looked at their reflections in the Venetian mirror that filled the wall opposite the windows. The mirror gave the illusion that it was a window revealing the clouds scuttling over the terrace's carved railings. Baron Belfort said the music room was a "riot of imagination" but Quantz had always thought the ornate decoration was a drunken brawl.

Columns of plaster divided the walls into large sections, leaving spaces for portraits, paintings, and scenes from Frederick's favorite operas, the ones his sister composed. The columns were more like tree trunks rising from the floor with their branches snaking across the ceiling to join at the chandelier. The plaster lines were covered in gold and silver to make them stand proud from the walls. They gave the impression of a frozen forest.

"And you will perform some miracle in wood?"

"Precisely. The gold will be matched by simple pine. The silver will be complemented by ash."

"So you will match the colors to the walls."

"To a point, but that will change."

Quantz could tell that Stephan was planning something more than a plain floor and looked over the plan on the table. His fingers traced the rigid symmetry of rectangles, squares, and lozenges on the paper. Everything was completely regular.

"How did you get everything to match?"

"Easy," Stephan crowed.

He showed Quantz little shapes sawn out of thin wood. He placed a square on the paper and scribed the edges with a dangerously sharp pencil. When he pulled up the guide, a perfect square nestled on the plan.

"I merely have to repeat the shapes to create the design."

"But here you have rectangles that are dark. I don't understand why."

Stephan smiled at his friend's confusion and at his own cunning. He felt a rare satisfaction in knowing something that evaded the Master of Music. He let the frustration simmer until Quantz had to ask, "Why do you have so much dark wood in this design?"

"Because the darkness holds the magic. Watch."

The room contained just enough gloom for Stephan to make his demonstration. He picked up a burning candle and cast its light over the paper, as if bathing a squirming infant. Instantly, the squares and lozenges rose before Quantz' eyes to become shapes in three dimensions. What had been flat plates was now a series of boxes. Under the waves of candle-light the design became steps rising to the walls and disappearing into the imagined distance.

Quantz stepped back to recreate the illusion shimmering on the paper. As he bent his body forward, Stephan's pencil lines jumped out in high relief, and as he bent back, the steps collapsed into flat, gray tracings.

"This will be intriguing," Quantz complimented. His eyes hovered between the table and the walls. The tops of the column destroyed the join between the walls and the ceiling, but the floor would flood over the border between the vertical and the horizontal.

"The eye plays tricks," Stephan bragged, "but I trick the eye."

Stephan basked in Quantz' genuine appreciation of his talent. Stephan was hatching a surprise.

"This is so exquisitely cunning," Quantz exclaimed with more than a suspicion of admiration.

"There was some lord in Russia," Stephan explained. "I think his name was Menshikov. This Menshikov liked playing tricks on his guests, so he had his peasants create a floor which gave the illusion that it was rising up as they walked over it. His friends were so startled that they tripped and fell down."

Quantz shared Stephan's mischievous grin, when he realized the trap Stephan was creating and did not disagree with the boast, "I will enjoy seeing the barons falling on their asses."

"The King will enjoy the game," Quantz assured him, "As long as he does not fall."

The room echoed with their breathing and Quantz savored the acoustics. When Stephan had completed his masterpiece, the room would assist him in both the composition and performance of the King's music. He had learned as a boy in the village band that every room not only had a voice of its own but also a temperature. He had mastered the ability to play very differently during practice in a cold church than when the building was filled with supplicants and sermons. The temperature changed according to the room's function and he had to adapt his playing accordingly. His knowledge of the necessity to comply with the laws of nature was no less vital if he were to survive the more subtle regulations of the court. There was safety in knowing the exact climate of a palace. Stephan's handiwork would ensure that his pupil's playing was always as accomplished as it was praiseworthy.

The stillness retreated under Stephan's heels marching over the floor. "You hear it?" he demanded with impatience. Quantz nodded sadly and Stephan continued his procession over the bare floorboards, grousing at every step.

"They just cast down planks of oak and called it a floor." His feet scuffed the boards below him and raised dust to his eyes. "At least they were all evenly planed," he conceded.

Quantz followed Stephan's footsteps, listening for the slightest variation in sound. They stopped to hear a wind gust rattle a window pane. They bent low and heard a tinkling between two planks.

"They pegged the boards to joists below," Stephan exclaimed with some heat, "but they didn't knock each plank together."

Quantz stood with his hands on his hips and sighed in resignation, "If this were the deck of a ship, it would sink in the first squall."

They watched the floorboards, searching for an answer, but the room was mute. "Can it be repaired?" Quantz asked in hope.

"We need more than repair. We must take this adversity and turn it to our advantage."

"I don't see how," Quantz said.

Stephan bounced to his work table and pulled out a long strip of material. Quantz immediately recognized it as one of Anna's sheets, cut into strips, three fingers wide. He cringed to think of what would happen when she discovered that her bedding had been purloined. He decided that discretion would be the better part of cowardice and he would tell her that some urchin probably stole it from her clothesline.

"I will have to caulk the space between each plank with linen. It will take weeks."

"I know just what you need," Quantz declared.

Quantz disappeared with an exaggerated curtsey and left Stephan to his labors and his confusion.

Those labors were becoming increasingly difficult for him, so he dragged himself back to the chair. Stephan was tired but his fatigue seemed to rise from his bones. He sat looking at his drawings and examining the area which they would inhabit. It was like mustering his troops for a bloodless attack on an empty territory. The floor seemed to mock his efforts to turn it into a thing as decorative as it was functional.

He rubbed his knees and coaxed relief into the swollen joints. Years of kneeling before these horizontal altars had taken their toll. There were some mornings that demanded he stay wrapped in night's warmth for the cold day was procession of irksome pains. Lately, he had noticed that shaking the sawdust from his hair left a streak of gray along the brown strands, like the shadow cast from a sundial. He sighed to think what would happen to him when his eyes were too dim to create the floors hardly anybody noticed twice.

The door opening roused him from gloomy speculations and Quantz led Heinz into the room.

"You now have an assistant," Quantz proclaimed.

Stephan grimaced his uncertainty and demanded if Heinz knew anything about carpentry.

"Yes, I know a lot about carpentry," Heinz answered.

"Such as what?" Stephan probed.

"Carpentry is all about wood."

"Anything else?"

"Sharp things."

Quantz laughed and told his friend, "The perfect apprentice."

Stephan sighed in resignation. "At least he will get me off my knees. Come here, boy."

Stephan threw one end of the ribbon to Heinz and dragged the line over the floor to the wall. Stephan knelt at the point farthest from the door and neatly tacked a nail into the head of the ribbon.

"What do you see?" he demanded of Heinz.

Heinz stroked his chin to mimic the court philosophers, hemmed and hawed as if discussing some obtuse concept with a learned colleague and reported, "The strip is held just over the join between two planks."

"Good. You are not blind. It is not a join because of the lazy idiot who put down the boards. We must turn these cracks into joins. Is there cloth on each side of the crack?"

Heinz inclined over the floorboards with his hands on his bent knees. "The cloth is as much on one board as it is on the other board."

"That is what we want. Get on your knees."

Stephan positioned Heinz so that one knee was on each side of the ribbon. "Now, pull gently but keep the ribbon very straight and tight." Heinz immediately obeyed and the ribbon jumped into a rigid line.

Stephan took a wide chisel, knelt with his rump almost in Heinz' face, and carefully positioned it on the ribbon just over the crack. He repeated his command for Heinz to pull the ribbon's free end, "tight," and knocked the chisel three times with a hammer.

Stephan crawled two paces backwards further down the ribbon and Heinz retreated in time with the master's knees. Stephan repeated his three knocks. Heinz saw the ribbon fold in the center and fill the crack. "More," Stephan demanded. Heinz dragged his knees backwards and Stephan followed him filling as they went along. Heinz soon picked up the rhythm and knew the purpose of what they were doing. Their four knees wiggled along the floor. They looked like a confused alligator, until they stood at the door.

"There," Stephan proclaimed with some pride, "that is how to caulk a floor."

Quantz and Heinz stood looking at the single white line running from the wall to the door. Stephan and Heinz had filled the space between two boards in much less time than Stephan could do on his own.

"What happens next?" Heinz inquired in his eagerness to please.

"We have to fill the entire floor before we do anything. The linen will keep the wood from squeaking when anybody walks on it."

"Won't the cloth come out?" Heinz asked.

"No, Boy. The cloth will be under the wood which will be the top of the floor."

"Then that wood will need more cloth."

"That wood, the top-wood will be glued to the floorboards and we will put down enough glue to fill any of the small holes the ribbon can't fill."

"So, it's like a big cake, just made of wood."

"That's about it."

Heinz picked up the hammer and volunteered to "work some more." Stephan immediately disarmed him. "First you learn about the wood. Then I'll let you play with the sharp things."

Stephan held the hammer by its head and hit Heinz' skull three times with the handle. Heinz protested the gentle assault, "I need my head."

"Only to hold up your hat," Stephan retorted.

Quantz saw the method in the rough instruction and laughed to hear Stephan explain. "Two taps," he demanded, as his forefinger banged on Heinz' skull "and one thump," as he struck the boy's forehead with the heel of his hand. Stephan reiterated the motion of finger and hand heel, all the while repeating, "Tap, Tap, Thump" until the patter was impressed on Heinz' memory and his scalp.

Stephan gave Quantz a satisfied nod to say that Heinz would do and that he appreciated the help that was as much a necessity as it was a relief.

Quantz watched Stephan and Heinz crawl backwards along the floor. He counted three hammer beats and a pause to each section of caulking forced into position. They were making rapid and rhythmic progress, and Quantz thought to himself, "I never realized he is so musical."

The hammering filled the music chamber and Quantz was glad that Stephan had returned to his concentrated efforts. Stephan was completely absorbed in his task and the intensity of the focus made Quantz question why Stephan was so intent whenever he was working or even thinking about work.

He had known Stephan for many years and valued the wide horizons of his knowledge and his judgments. He had views on everything, but Quantz had come to know that Stephan also had facts to support his opinions. They had spent many an evening in heated discussion and Quantz had laughed at Stephan's vapors, until he understood the wisdom he had so painfully acquired. Could it be that Stephan's life was sickened by the panorama of his life kneeling in a multitude of courts? Lately, there had crept into his conversation a tone of constant disgust. It was more than the usual grousing of servants. This was something toxic that must be avoided. There were few antidotes to cynicism. Stephan had relinquished most of his hopes, knowing that disappointment is always the proud parent of despair.

Now, Quantz saw Stephan lose himself in the details of his trade. He was more concerned with the grain of a piece of wood than with the arcane debates of the king's philosophers. Indeed, he had confessed to Quantz that the deliberations of the likes of de la Metrie and all the rest of the "brains crowned in imperial laurels" left him cold. Quantz had tried to tease Stephan's temper by referring to Belfort's much praised and never read thesis. Stephan had just shrugged his shoulders and dismissed the Baron's flights of intellectual fancy as "just enough salon chatter to put one to sleep." Quantz loved Stephan's dismissal of such pretentious postulations as "just another powder for an insomniac." He had laughed at Stephan's pronouncement that the philosophers' concepts were merely, "Big boys' games that go nowhere and have absolutely no meaning or relevance to reality."

But there was more than annoyance in Stephan's responses. There was a deep fear and a retreat from everything the court represented. Hammering a nail or cutting a groove to the highest level of his skill was now much more important to him than any abstraction demanding his attention and intruding upon his work. Quantz saw that Stephan was seeking a refuge in these simple accomplishments. He was finding the angels in the details.

Quantz very carefully let himself out of the music room and silently closed the door behind him. Now that he understood the importance of Stephan's firmness of purpose and his desperate need for focus, Quantz refused to disturb his friend's composed tranquility. What was so clear that it could no longer be denied by Quantz was the simple fact that his friend was getting old.

Chapter 10

Duet

Defutois took his place outside the music room. He had timed his duties with the king's pen to coincide with the royal flute lesson. Defutois had fallen into the habit of accompanying Quantz and spent the time listening at the door. Quantz did not object to his companion for he knew that Defutois was listening attentively. He was always ready to answer Defutois' eager questions about whatever he had heard.

He had confessed to Quantz that he was an illiterate with music but wished to vanquish his ignorance because of Quantz' playing. The hour or so he waited for his turn at the King's table was well spent in listening to the music. Quantz always left the door slightly ajar, so that Defutois could hear the music. He had asked, "Do you not become bored with the constant repetition of just a few notes?" Defutois assured him, "A few notes at a time is all I can handle."

So it was with some anticipation that Defutois lounged alertly in the corridor. He sometimes felt like a voyeur stealing glances of a frantic coupling, but the dictionary he carried in his mind assured him that 'voyeur' was a trick of the eye and there was no corresponding word for a treat for the ear. He relaxed into whatever musical gifts Quantz would allow to escape the room.

Quantz and Frederick were playing one of Frederick's duets. This composition was similar to all the others Frederick had jotted down. When he found some notes appealing to his taste, he would cast a sheet to Quantz to turn it into something he could play. Quantz could accomplish such tasks in a matter of minutes, but he always delayed the delivery because "a task quickly performed is never appreciated." He would wait a few days until Frederick had completely forgotten about his ditty and then present the finished product. Frederick was overjoyed by the reminder and grasped each of Quantz' labors as a gift, all the more desired because it was so unexpected. When he played through Quantz' improvements of his notes, Frederick was always pleased by how good his music sounded. "You have so skillfully brought out the essential beauty of the bare notes," he had praised, and Quantz had bowed deeply in appreciation of the compliment.

Defutois could make out some of the words over the music, but the conversation was always like listening to a stream in gentle flood. The tone was always calm, even if some of the words conveyed a more harsh feeling. After weeks of purloining notes and snatches of sentences, Defutois had a sensation that the music lesson was merely an excuse for something else, something which evaded his comprehension, but which he was determined to acquire. The sounds all had feeling, whether in the music or in the words, but the meanings were as elusive as they were obscure to him. At his post by the door, he frequently perceived that he was juggling clouds.

Quantz had no such problems. The years of teaching Frederick had inured him to the vagaries of his position. It had been quite some time since Frederick had surrendered to one of his monumental fits of temper over the slightest suggestion that he play a trill in a more mature manner. The first time it happened Quantz was terrified by the storm of foul temper and fouler words spat at him. He had remained calm, as if before an enraged animal, and had stepped back until the tempest had subsided. Frederick had never apologized, indeed, he seemed to have forgotten any such incident. Quantz realized that he could also feign a loss of memory, but he never forgot the lesson. His face was always a mask of serenity, even when his mind was raging with the possible consequences of Frederick's fit. His only protection was the flute he held.

Frederick lurched forward to translate the black dots on the paper before him into sounds that filled the room. Quantz stepped back and sagely stroked his chin, waiting for the torrent to end. With a final clipping of his breath, Frederick finished his performance and looked to Quantz for both guidance and assurance, but mainly the latter. Quantz was quick to observe, "you have chosen a very tricky approach to this line, but your talent is such as to make the selection most suitable." Frederick beamed at the acknowledgement of his expertise and nodded in submissive agreement with Quantz' analysis. "But how can it be made even better?" he demanded.

"Although it may sound like a contradiction, you are asking me 'How does one improve on perfection?' and I would be duty bound to say let the music lead you."

Frederick had heard this advice so often that it was almost a section of his musical catechism. He waited attentively for instruction, and the King's silence was the permission for Quantz to instruct.

Quantz pointed his flute to the center of the page of notation, "Here would be a good place to start." He blew three notes and made sure they were all equal in duration and volume. "Three simple notes, but the music is lurking midst the trio." He played them again and Frederick cocked an attentive ear to his teacher's instrument. He heard Quantz play the notes with the regularity of a mill wheel perpetually rotating. "But even something as simple as three notes offers us the possibilities of variation," he shared.

"How does one vary something so small?" Frederick asked with genuine enquiry and patient attendance upon the answer.

"With accent," Quantz commanded.

Quantz blew the notes and his breath hit the first note to make it stand proud from the other two. "We have worked on tone," Frederick complained. "And you have mastered the tonal qualities of each note of all the scales you have so assiduously practiced," Quantz graciously conceded.

Frederick squinted, as if sensing a trap, so Quantz was quick to snap it shut. "You have a beautiful tone, so now you can apply that tone to the sections of the music you wish to emphasize." Quantz repeated the phrase with added emphasis on the first note. "Since you are the master of tone, you can choose where to apply that skill." Quantz again repeated the trio of sounds, but this time, his breath struck on the third note with exaggerated force. Frederick's ears heard the truth of Quantz' advice, but he was apprehensive of his own abilities to turn the advice into reality.

Quantz sensed Frederick's insecurity and let it simmer. He knew any innovation in the music would turn Frederick into a skittish horse, balking at a jump. When he felt Frederick groping for the chance to play, Quantz wielded his flute like a whip and demanded, "Play the notes three times with the stress on the first note and immediately play them three more times with the accent on the last note."

Frederick obeyed, but he sprayed timidity over the note. Quantz remained silent, for he knew that interrupting his master's attempts to please him could be the fuze to great unpleasantness. Frederick continued to the end and rested the flute upon his chest.

"That is excellent. Now let us play it together."

They raised their instruments and followed the steps in unison. Quantz delicately stressed the first accent and accompanied Frederick thumping the note as if he were playing the bass drum in the regimental band. By the time they approached the last set, Frederick's confidence had grown to the point where he could just touch the correct hole on the flute and make the accent as clear as it was subdued. They listened for a moment to the echoing silence.

"That is how one stresses at the beginning or at the end of a phrase. Now you are playing it with command and with the sensitivity that your music demands."

Frederick's chest expanded with his achievement and Quantz knew this was the invitation for more. With each repetition, Quantz stoked Frederick's need for validation through music.

"Now, let us move up the scale to the next three notes," and he signaled for them to continue their duet. The fingers of Frederick's left hand jumped to release the sounds, but he kept the same accents as Quantz had taught him. They repeated the exercise three more times, and Quantz stopped to allow Frederick's breath to catch up with his enthusiasm.

"Let us now vary the accent. Strong on the first note, subdued and even-tempered in the center, and extremely strong but not too loud on the last note." Frederick obeyed and Quantz smiled his approval at the six notes held together into one phrase by the two accents. It sounded so much better to Frederick, and he reveled in his achievement under Quantz' gentle touch. "Think of it like a few books held in place by two bookends. Each note now stands straight, with volumes of promise." Frederick could not resist playing the phrase again, and Quantz was happy to indulge his eager application.

Quantz remembered General Katte relating one of his many, and less tedious, anecdotes of Prince Frederick. During a battle, Frederick ordered the Guard forward and followed them on horseback almost to the bayonet points of the enemy. Frederick had calmly taken out his flute and was practicing his scales in the very center of the slaughter and well within range of the enemy's guns. But he serenely sat his horse, quietly playing his scales. To Quantz, such aplomb hinted at insanity. To be so absorbed in a few notes when, at any moment, a musket ball could tear out your brain, revealed either a firm belief in a beneficent Fate or a complete indifference to life. Whatever had happened on that flesh sodden field, the mere fact of the practice of scales demonstrated that the flute was some sort of Guardian Angel to a very complicated mind. Perhaps there was some magic in this wooden tube which had evaded Quantz all these years. Or perhaps Frederick was just crazy.

Knowing the comfort Frederick derived from scales, he encouraged him to continue the same accent exercise in different keys. Frederick offered the excuse that he had not practiced some of those scales in a very long time, so Quantz assured him, "No matter. The repetition gives the fingers the power of memory. If you make mistakes, the error is just like reminding your hands how to produce the notes. It will all come back."

Frederick bumbled his way through ladders of sound until he was hitting every note in its proper place along its defined sequence, but he was also placing the accents where Quantz demanded.

"Now," Quantz said when he had allowed Frederick to finish, "it is time that we progressed over the next three lines."

Relieved of scale duty, Frederick bounded through half a page of his composition and stopped to regain his breath. They stood gazing at the black dots before them, and Frederick felt as though they were sneering at him. "The piece will benefit from the accents," he admitted ruefully.

Fredrick played through the piece again and the accents jumped in his ear. He rested the flute and squinted at the notes. They seemed to rise from the paper and stand before his eyes. He looked again, and the notes stood distinct from the stave, waiting to be played. "You are right. There are places I have completely missed," he confessed.

"Even genius needs memory," Quantz assured him, and Frederick guffawed at the effrontery of the back-handed compliment. "Let us then exercise memory. The fingers will remember with diligent practice."

Together, they played to the end of the page. Frederick stood on the precipice of frustration and sighed, "There is something missing."

Quantz knew exactly what was evading Frederick's suspicion of incompleteness and made a great play of considering the notes. When Frederick couldn't stand any more of such contemplation, Quantz quietly said, "the horse."

"The horse?" Frederick almost begged in surprise.

"Yes, the horse." Quantz repeated.

"Master of Music," Frederick blurted, "you are being purposely obtuse. Enough of this teasing… Reveal."

Quantz delayed obedience to the royal command and pointedly thrust his flute to the paper. "Here," he exclaimed, "there should be a horse."

"What type of horse?" Frederick demanded with the hint of pique.

"Oh, any horse will do. But I would suggest a spirited hunter."

Now that he had Frederick firmly under his control, he explained in simple detail.

"Your music has a natural tendency to run ahead of itself. There is a pacing to your notes, the same as is in the breast of any well-bred beast. As the hunter so desires to have his head, so too does your composition yearn to be set free. Observe."

Quantz played through the piece, careful to place the accents exactly where they were most needed and with just the right emphasis for Frederick to distinctly hear them. When Frederick recognized the proper accent, he greeted each with a welcoming and relieved nod of his head. Quantz played with one eye on the notes and the other on Frederick. He got to the end and asked, "Now, what do you hear?"

"Accents and they seem to separate the music."

"When you play them, the accents will join the music."

He played again and Frederick could hear each distinct section separated by the slightest accent in Quantz' performance.

"I still don't see this horse of which you speak," he complained.

"That is because I have not yet released him from his comfortable stable." He could sense Frederick getting frustrated and decided it was time to cast aside the reins. He pointed to different places along the lines of notes.

"The horse must be paced. Walk, march, trot, must precede the gallop, if the horse is not to be blown before arriving as its destination."

Quantz played it again, but with the accents rising from a low, almost lugubrious, tempo to a confident and steady pace, to end at a thrilling and breath-taking finalé. Frederick now heard the horse and was astounded by the simple mastery of Quantz' few notes. He wanted desperately to emulate this playing and Quantz sensed the earnestness of the student bursting through the restraint of the King.

Frederick copied Quantz' performance and repeated it until he felt increased command of the instrument. Quantz counted through the piece with his flute and then tucked it under his arm to applaud Frederick. "Bravo. Bravo. This is exactly what you want for your composition."

"It certainly sounds much more... more... animated," Frederick said with a thrill. "But there still seems to be something missing."

"Not in the music," Quantz observed.

"Then where?"

"In the stance."

Frederick's shuffled his feet in uncertainty and waited for Quantz' explanation.

"You play the flute with the fingers and the mouth. The body is to support the music."

"Should not my movements follow the music?" Frederick protested.

"Only if you are a dancer."

Quantz stood relaxed with one hand on his hip. "Put your left foot forward at a slight angle to the right foot."

Frederick placed his feet to mimic Quantz' stance.

"Now, place the flute at a right angle to the mouth."

Frederick stood rigid as a mannequin which had just been shot in the face with an arrow.

"Now, sound one note."

Frederick blew and the note filled the room.

"That sounds much fuller," Frederick sighed.

"That is because you are assuming a position to liberate the air."

Frederick agreed and straightened his torso as Quantz decreed.

"Your feet should be in the same position as a rather moderate "en guard." As you must stand to wield the blade, so too you must stand to allow the flute to make the music. Observe."

Quantz assumed his habitual stance and his flute flooded the room to the ceiling, vanquishing the sound left by Frederick's single note.

"The feet support the body, so the chest is free to breathe into the instrument."

Frederick rose to his full height and sent another full note, pregnant with rich overtones.

"The flute should be balanced between the thumbs of the right and left hands." Frederick fumbled his fingers into this more dexterous grasp. "Gently support the instrument in the crook between your thumb and index finger," Quantz commanded. Frederick obeyed and could feel his flute nestle into his hands. He tested the position with another booming note, until Quantz corrected him. "There is no need to press so forcefully to the mouth. The chin should lift and fall to raise and lower the tone. Do not hold the flute as if it were a musket and bayonet."

Frederick breathed deeply to relax and stood with his fingers poised to play. The new grip made him anxious that the flute would fall from his hands to the floor. He tensed to avoid such a catastrophe but continued to play the passage with exaggerated motions.

"You need not squirm as you play," Quantz interrupted, "You should not sway, for you are playing with your fingers, not with your shoulders."

"Would not the expression of the face and the movement of the body enhance the performance?"

"Such gyrations and grimaces are very suitable for a Polish fifer or a French courtesan. But you are a German king."

Quantz knew this last statement would fill Frederick's lungs, so he made him play again and force any indignation through the flute rather than at Quantz. It was time for the coup de grace.

"Your Majesty is replete with musical whimsy. It would be such a waste of talent and such a loss to culture if you were filled with the noisome gears and annoying cogs of Monsieur Vaucanson."

Frederick bowed his complete capitulation, and Quantz knew that the halls of the court would never again echo with the accursed name of Vaucanson.

Quantz made him play through the piece again with the accents, the tone, the pace, and the stance. Frederick felt the results were something of a miracle and beamed his gratitude at his teacher.

"Quantz" Frederick started with clear admiration in his voice, "that is quite amazing. What generated such improvement?"

"You have created wonderful music on paper. But the five lines of the stave can also be the bars of a prison. With the simplest of solutions, we have solved the most complex of problems. From your feet, to your chest, to your tongue, you have liberated the music from the notes."

They rested for a few moments. Frederick played with the flute and Quantz bided his time. When he judged the right moment had arrived, he very calmly suggested, "May we continue into the next section?"

"Do you think it is necessary?"

"Nothing outside your will is necessary. But now that the first page is so complete, the music begs a continuance. Just a few more bars, as they are so beautiful."

Quantz had copied the notes, so he knew exactly what would come next. He encouraged Frederick to slightly quicken the pace, and when he turned the page, the sound died.

Frederick stopped abruptly and looked at his flute. "Is there a problem?" Quantz asked nonchalantly.

"Either there is something wrong with this flute or my teeth are falling out."

Quantz blinked at the page and pointed with his flute. "Play that note," he commanded.

Frederick obeyed and the note rang clear. "Now the next," Quantz encouraged. Frederick depressed the lever on the foot joint with the small finger of his right hand, and the flute burped.

"Now play the notes as slowly as possible, "Quantz commanded.

Quantz listened as if he were a physician checking his patient's breathing, his ear searching for any wheeze that could suggest a greater problem. "Again," he said, and Frederic's fingers rose and fell, his little finger working the lever of the D key.

"May I inspect this disobedient child?" Quantz almost begged, and Frederick handed him his flute.

Quantz pressed the key in the flute's foot-joint and played the same notes. A quick glance revealed that the leather pad under the lever was worn down, paper thin, and was not closing the hole. He very carefully manipulated the lever so that it would make a hissing noise.

"Do you hear that?" he asked.

"Why, yes," Frederick agreed with as much interest as disappointment. "It sounds as if it has gas."

Quantz played again and made the flute hiss like a snake. He then pronounced, "The problem is not in the music, for that is beautiful. It is the instrument."

"Can it be repaired?" Frederick asked.

"I fear that it has come to the end of its natural life."

Frederick gazed at his flute with all the regret he would feel if he had to shoot one of his dogs.

"What is to be done?" he whined.

"I have foreseen this very problem."

Frederick's eyes brightened with renewed vigor, and Quantz explained.

"You have simply progressed in playing beyond the capabilities of this instrument. This flute is worn out."

"But can the instrument be saved?"

"It should be replaced with another, more suitable to your talents."

Frederick's eyes shone like a child anticipating a longed for Christmas. Quantz stood relaxed, confident he was the bearer of gifts to please a king.

"You suggest that I have a new flute?" Frederick beamed.

"Not just any flute. I have been working on something quite new and extraordinary and I must thank Your Majesty for being the cause of these new innovations to the instrument."

Frederick's full attention was focused on Quantz.

"Your Majesty, has given me the high honor of placing your confidence in a good master. You are the student with the genuine desire to perfect himself, who discovers from time-to-time, new benefits he had been previously unable to perceive."

He paused to allow the words to seep past Frederick's defenses and invade his vanity.

"If there is no deliberation and reflection in music it is merely a pastime without profit."

Frederick felt as if he were being berated by a strict schoolmaster, unaware of the high station of his pupil, but waited for more.

"In this respect a noble pride must prevent the beginner from being easily satisfied and must inspire him to gradually perfect himself.

"Anyone who only cares to devote himself to music haphazardly, as to a trade rather than an art, will forever remain a lifelong bungler."

"When will we welcome this happy occasion?"

"I beg your indulgence and you patience for a further month, for this next flute will necessitate a complete renewal of the art."

"Must I wait a month?" Frederick whined.

"The delay is determined by my quarters." Quantz sighed.

"Is your accommodation insufficient for your duties?"

"They are most generous for myself and my family, but the addition of a small workshop would be most convenient."

"Then add another room to your house."

"I fear such an undertaking is beyond my means."

"Nonsense," Frederick guffawed, "We have the Chancellor to deal with such things."

Quantz did not need the dismissive wave of Frederick's hand to know that their lesson was finished. He bowed to Frederick and took his leave. Frederick stood practicing his piece, confident that the error was in his hands and not in his music.

As he turned into the corridor, he saw Defutois' back heaving as he gulped down great quantities of air and hissed it out of his mouth. He was standing "en guarde" in the same position Frederick had assumed under Quantz' tutelage. Quantz tapped him on the shoulder and Defutois jumped in embarrassment to be discovered in his little game of mimicry.

Quantz bowed deeply and ironically, and exclaimed, "Euterpe gives way to Thalia." Defutois looked confused until Quantz said, "The muse of music surrenders to the muse of comedy." Defutois felt a fool for forgetting such a simple allusion to Classical literature but returned the bow and entered the music room.

Quantz walked down the corridor. with a smile quavering upon his satisfied lips. He amused himself with some mental arithmetic. "Subtract one Vaucanson," he grinned in righteous malice. "Add one new flute for two hundred golden florins." He laughed to envision the coins rattling in his moneybox. "Add an extra room at no cost." The relief flooded his cheeks when he mused, "Minus one new dresser for forty florins." Anna would be so pleased at the prospect of the new furniture and he would take renewed pride in his true function of provider for the family fortunes. "There will even be enough left over for some Dutch crockery."

His steps tapped out the rhythm of Frederick's dreadful dirge and he savored his success, for it had been a most profitable duet.

Chapter 11

Aria

Quantz marched the corridors of the palace with determination but also with restrained haste. Quickened footsteps on marble always signaled opportunity to courtiers ever-vigilant for advantage. His years as a blacksmith had taught him to strike while the iron is hot, but also that each blow must be strong and precise. Even hammering a horseshoe demanded an art denied to the eager novice. The king's memory soon faded but accounts in the ledgers of the Treasury were permanent. The Chancellor was always most assiduous in fulfilling the King's wishes, even if those desires were as simple as an extra room in a servant's quarters.

He walked the pavements until he arrived at the administrative building and proceeded to the private chambers of the Chancellor. Krause, the Chancellor's secretary, looked up from his desk, saw Quantz patiently waiting, and immediately stood to greet him. Quantz asked if he "could be so bold as to beg a few moments of the Chancellor's precious time." Krause was happy to oblige, for Quantz was one of the few favored servants who asked and never demanded. The secretary was also happy to receive a little unsolicited charm, for Quantz' habitual and kindly, if somewhat distant, manner was more appreciated than the peremptory commands secretaries were usually afforded. "Of course, Maestro. I am sure the Chancellor will be delighted."

Quantz did not have to wait very long for Krause to usher him into the Chancellor's presence. He bowed in exaggerated irony and stood defiantly relaxed. "My Dear Quantz," the Chancellor fussed, "we can dispense with tedious ceremony."

The Chancellor sat in his chair as if it were a throne, but his leg rested on a cushioned footstool.

"You join me in the hour of my postprandial stupor," the Chancellor sighed.

"I take it you have had a most satisfying repast," Quantz said.

"The pleasures of the table account for both my gout and my gas. The former affords me a sedentary existence and the latter keeps me safe from courtiers. Please, take a seat."

Quantz smiled and sat. The Chancellor's conversation was always as amusing as his manner was delightful. Quantz admired the great bulk filling the chair. The man's genuine love of music and his intelligent interest in all aspects of the art could not be hidden behind the half-closed lid of his lazy left eye. Sometimes Quantz mused that the Chancellor was a well-fed seal in court dress, who would much prefer to be sitting at the opera.

Quantz sat attentively and politely refused the Chancellor's offer of a tray of bonbons.

"I must decline, Your Excellency," Quantz exclaimed. "Chocolate has a most deleterious effect on my throat and I must be very careful to maintain control of my breath, if I am to perform."

"Quite right, Quantz," the Chancellor agreed, "and we must keep that throat in its best condition, if we are to have the joy you provide through that throat."

Quantz smiled his thanks and sat politely silent.

"So, what brings you to my lair?" inquired the Chancellor.

"His Majesty has suggested that my quarters be expanded and that I discuss the particulars with yourself."

"I have the very man for such matters," and he shouted, "Krause."

Krause appeared as if from a cloud and awaited his instructions. The Chancellor waved his bloated and ringed fingers to his secretary and commanded, "Send some masons to Quantz' house."

"The masons are all occupied with the new stables," Krause reminded the Chancellor, who mused for a few seconds.

"Horses are very patient beasts, except when they are being slaughtered."

"I will attend to this immediately," Krause said and evaporated from the room.

This is one time when Quantz was thankful for Prussian efficiency for he knew that the suggestions of the monarch were the commands of the subject.

"Thank you so much for such speedy execution of the King's desires," he said.

"It is our duty to serve a kindly master and our pleasure to extend his largesse. But enough of bricks and wood."

Quantz was prepared for the Chancellor's continuance.

"Please allow me to thank you for the magnificent concert you gave us last week. I was particularly struck by the cadenza. What a lovely surprise and a treat. You have an extraordinary gift."

"The result of many years of somewhat tedious practice."

"Tell me," the Chancellor leaned toward his listener, "I have heard many such performances but your mastery of the instrument surpasses all others. Is there a secret to such alchemy?"

"There is no secret to music, as you yourself readily realize."

"But how is it that you can produce such beauty from, please forgive my ignorance, a stick of wood?"

"You are Italian, so you have the knowledge already."

"Is the magic in the Italian tongue?" the Chancellor teased.

"To an extent," Quantz considered. "It is in the Italian voice."

"You are playing with me, Quantz. Let me not burst in curiosity."

"The French perform in a manner which is pleasing to the individual player, but they are completely deficient when playing with each other. The leader of a French orchestra should use a whip rather than a baton."

"So, conducting French musicians is like herding cats. We know that. But what does this have to do with an Italian?"

"You have heard many wonderful voices in your native land."

"All of such voices."

"There are two Italian voices which rise to the heights of art but do not destroy the ears with their shrieking," Quantz declaimed.

"And these are?"

"Angeletta and Farinelli."

The Chancellor clasped his paws together at the mention of old friends. "You know them both?"

"Professionally," Quantz admitted but was quick to add, "not intimately."

"I heard Angelleta in Venice. I can still hear her ala Pieta. Another girl played the violin," the Chancellor reminisced.

"Precisely. I heard her also in Venice."

"She had been brought up in an orphanage," the Chancellor remembered, "but she married a banker."

"She had such a beautiful voice," Quantz recalled. "Strong in singing as well as playing on the clavier."

"How can her singing initiate me into the mysteries of your flute?" the Chancellor queried.

"It is quite simple. What is the difference between Angelleta and a fishwife?"

The Chancellor's curiosity was enlivened by a riddle he so enjoyed and he spent some time devising his response.

"I was never that close to Angelleta, but I have been informed the fishwife smells better."

"A good start," Quantz admitted. "Now imagine that Angelleta is singing on the stage and the fishwife is scolding her husband. What is the difference?"

"Angelleta would probably not attack her husband with a fish."

"More especially since her husband can protect himself from her assaults with his wealth. Angelleta would attack with words and music but she would sing the same notes that the fishwife would howl."

"This fishwife of yours," the Chancellor prodded, "has she been trained in the vocal arts?"

"Never. She must rely on the organs nature gave her."

"So, Angelleta's organs have been trained to art, while the fishwife is tuned to nature."

"But they both have the same emotions," Quantz thrust back.

"So the singer is merely performing by the mimicry of her art what this harridan accomplishes only by the force of her own passion."

"They both have the passion. A good singer delivers the notes in a pleasing manner. A great singer gives us the sense of the words with the music. Our ears are delighted as our minds are enlightened. To sing without sense is to imitate a chicken laying an egg."

"Quantz, even if your were to perform on a chicken, your music would never befoul us."

"That would be sauce for the goose," Quantz quipped.

The Chancellor's chortled at Quantz' repartee, which gave him time to consider his next move.

"But to move from the ridiculous to the sublime, the flute has no words," the Chancellor observed.

"True, but what it lacks in vocabulary is supplied with the feeling of the music. Without the words, the flute player must do double duty. He must have all the beauty of the sound, but being deprived of the words, the flute must evoke the emotions of the missing words."

"You are saying that the flutist is a poet without words," the Chancellor added with teasing skepticism.

"In a manner," Quantz conceded. "Angelleta and the fishwife would berate their spouses using exactly the same notes. The flute has only the notes. It is really a singer with the feeling that brings forth the sense."

"This is wonderful," the Chancellor conceded.

"Think of a well-prepared meal. The singer with mediocre talent can deliver the sounds but not the fullness of the song. Such musicians are like chefs who can only prepare sauces and forget the meat. The sauce only satisfies when the meat is fresh."

"I have heard that Farenelli is a most saucy fellow."

"But there is such substance to his meat," Quantz recalled.

"The magnificence, the power of his voice. Such a wonder is worth the sacrifice of his manhood," the Chancellor jibed.

"Farinelli's voice is well-carrying, so well-rounded, rich and strong. High, even a soprano voice."

The Chancellor lounged into his recollection of wonders he could never forget. Quantz saw the look of sadness shudder over the Chancellor's brow and wanted to smooth those wrinkled cares with conversation.

"His intonation is pure," Quantz' pronounced to the Chancellor's delight. "His trillo beautiful, his chest unusually strong in the long holding of notes. His throat is very flexible so he can sing the largest intervals with the greatest ease and the firmest certainty."

The Chancellor was overjoyed to investigate such arcane aspects of music and Quantz was willing to supply such comfort.

"But what do Italian singers have to do with a German flute player?" the Chancellor asked with growing curiosity.

"I play the flute as Angelleta and Farenelli sing their songs, and only rarely in practice as the fishwife shrieks."

"So what I am hearing you play is really an aria without words."

"Yes, to a certain extent."

"But how can it be an aria without the words to give us the sense of what is being sung?"

"You say that your emotions are moved in the opera?"

"Most certainly," the Chancellor confessed.

"But is it the meaning of the words which move you so?"

"Yes. I can experience the poetry with the music."

"But what if the words were not needed?" Quantz asked.

"I do not understand."

"Would you have the same joy if the singer declaimed the poetry in Chinese, or in any other language you could not comprehend?"

"You are losing me again."

"When the poem is declaimed properly is there not a rhythm to the words?"

"Of course there is."

"Then we can say that the poetry produces music."

The Chancellor mused over Quantz digging into his most treasured pleasure and was willing to reveal his own confusion.

"The music produced by the declamation of beautiful words stirs your emotions?"

The Chancellor listened attentively to Quantz articulating the thoughts he almost feared to express. He was eager for more of the master's wisdom, for attending to Quantz was like listening to himself.

"Now dispense with the words. Do you still have the feelings of the music when the poetry is purged of its words?"

"That is most certainly the case," the Chancellor agreed, as if hearing this idea for the first time.

"What is left is what I play on the flute. The sounds of the music evoke the emotions, those same emotions brought forth by the poem."

The Chancellor sat back and raised his chin, as if digesting these exciting thoughts served with such exquisite delicacy.

"Playing the flute is a song without words," the Chancellor exclaimed and Quantz was quick to cap the thought, "Playing the flute with no emotions is soulless garbage."

Quantz' eyes followed the gleam of satisfaction blossoming in the Chancellor's cheeks. Their discourse was thrilling to the Chancellor, but Quantz was sensing a feeling beneath the words. There was the merest suggestion of discomfort in the Chancellor's expression. When they had previously spoken of music, the Chancellor was like an eager student, yearning for more of the master's knowledge. On this occasion, it seemed to Quantz that the satisfaction of understanding was only fueling some other, some inner pain upon which it would be both presumptuous and unkind to intrude.

"Your analogy between music and saucy meat is most intriguing. But I must confess there is much rottenness beneath the sauce."

"Now I am the one to be lost, Your Excellency."

"I doubt it," the Chancellor said, "but let us look at your comparison of a musical performance to a well prepared meal. No amount of sauce can disguise the rot below, if the meat is putrid."

"I suspect you speak of more than table menus."

"The meal is but an aperitif. It is Rameau which troubles me."

"Rameau. The Composer to the King of France?"

"The same."

Quantz was perplexed by the Chancellor's sudden and clearly intense interest in the music of Rameau. The quiet dignity of those ballets and the keyboard works had enthralled Quantz since he first heard them. 'Rameau' in this discussion felt like bait in one of the Chancellor's debating traps.

"I cannot recall anything in Rameau's music which could either give offense or trouble the mind," Quantz confessed.

"It is not in the music but in the libretto where the trouble lurks."

"You are back to music and poetry."

"To the meaning behind both," the Chancellor said.

"Just where do you find a problem?"

The Chancellor sat back and paused to allow Quantz to both ponder the question and to simmer in confusion. When he felt he had Quantz stumped, he crossed his arms over his chest and questioned very softly. "Do you remember Rameau's masterpiece *Les Indes Galantes*?"

"Rameau has created so many masterpieces that it is difficult to distinguish."

Quantz was nudged off balance by the Chancellor's very sudden intrusion of Rameau's opera into their conversation. He had seen this opera on his tour of Europe, many decades in the past. He had only the most fleeting memory of the opera's action but he could never forget the music. The play seemed to be seared into the Chancellor's mind and the vehemence of his words told Quantz that there was something important for the Chancellor in this magnificent but forgotten tale.

The Chancellor continued to speak, but his voice was distant, obscured by Quantz' desperation to remember. His mind hooked onto the first few bars of Émilie's aria and the stage appeared in his mind. The music heralded a procession of dancers emerging from a theatrical ocean. The story was the usual ensemble of implausible situations and absurd characters. Osman, the lusty and dusky Turkish pasha drags the virtuous, French, voluptuous, and oh so white Émile to his harem. As the virgin is about to be ravished, Valère, her true love appears. Osman, out of the goodness of his heart, frees the two lovers, and all sing a trio in praise of chaste love. All very moral, and to Quantz' mind, laughable.

"I will not insult you with a recitation of the entire story. A minor incident will suffice to explain the whole," the Chancellor said to Quantz' relief.

Quantz, his memory refreshed, waited for the Chancellor's next lunge.

"Remember when the two lovers, Valère and Émilie are freed?"

"Yes. It is a most touching scene," Quantz remembered.

"They are in the clutches of Osman, but this pasha has both a heart and a conscience, so he frees both Émilie, after whom he lusts, and her lover, Valère, to whom he is indebted."

Quantz sighed and assured the Chancellor that the scene was in his mind as if it were performed only yesterday, even though it had taken such effort to recall even these slight details. But it was the details that trapped the Chancellor's attention.

"This Osman," the Chancellor stabbed a forefinger to Quantz' face, "this Turk, relinquishes the satisfactions of the flesh to unite two lovers."

"That is most surprising," Quantz said.

"Is not the freeing of the slave a noble act?" the Chancellor asked.

"Most truly." Quantz agreed. "But this particular act of Osman is very curious."

"Then you will appreciate the problem in this extraordinary scene," the Chancellor said.

"Osman has acted most nobly in liberating his servants," Quantz said.

"But he has also returned their goods along with their slaves."

"That is just part of the story," Quantz added.

"But do you not see the irony in celebrating a liberation with gifts of bondage?"

The Chancellor had laid a very neat trap for Quantz. All his appeal to the beauties of music were lost, if the music only served as a cover for brutality.

"It is a story," Quantz exclaimed, restraining the heat from his voice. "We should not delve too deeply to discover truths which are not there."

"It is a parable," the Chancellor retorted. "We must delve, if we are to fathom the meaning."

Quantz suddenly realized what had happened. The Chancellor had turned the tables on him. Instead of presenting the music of emotion, he had dredged up a meaning full of emotion to confront the music. Quantz had to admit the dexterity of the mind that could play such tricks and still remain calm in the execution of his enquiring tactics. Quantz would have to be on his guard if the Chancellor ever invited him to a game of chess.

"In such a situation is not the music sauce for the rotten meat? A thing of beauty is reduced to mere camouflage for cruelty?" the Chancellor asked.

"It can be," Quantz agreed, "just as anything of good and beauty can be turned to evil and ugliness."

"So, the music cannot make us moral?" the Chancellor thought aloud.

"One becomes good by choosing good," Quantz reflected. "A murderer may sing like Angelleta while stabbing you in the back. The fault is in he who wields the knife and not in the song he sings."

The Chancellor exploded into applause and clasped his hands together. "Bravo, Maestro, Bravo."

Quantz understood that he had won the argument without beating his opponent. The Chancellor had that magnanimity of character that could concede without taking the concession as an affront to his dignity. Quantz admired the Chancellor's ability to separate his vanity from his intellect. He truly did love to understand and in that love there was humility before the subject and respect for the teacher. Their intellectual fencing was subtle because it was dedicated to understanding and not to conquest or submission. If someone ran the Chancellor through with a foil, even if it were possible to pierce such bulk, his last words would be "Bravo. Well played."

The Chancellor smiled at Quantz, as if he were a child unwrapping a long coveted gift. There was a kindliness to his face that spoke to Quantz and a sweetness to the voice as inviting as it was clear.

"As ever, Quantz, you enlighten me."

"I merely draw forth what you already know. A man without your taste could never benefit from such instruction."

Quantz returned the smile with an assurance that his compliment was not mere etiquette but the sincerity of a friend.

"He would be too ignorant?" the Chancellor inquired.

"He would be too arrogant," Quantz finished.

Quantz heard more than acquiescence in the voice. There was appreciation. The Chancellor had craved their exchange of ideas, but there was a hint of desperation to his enthusiasm. This was no gentleman's jousting with words. The Chancellor seemed to be exercising a memory grown weak with years. Quantz surmised that the Chancellor feared his age was capturing his mind. Whatever the man needed, Quantz would supply to the utmost of his ability. He would not repay the kindness of years with the greed of a few days. He would leave that to all the others who would find some advantage in the Chancellor's predicaments.

That was when the thought erupted in Quantz' mind. The Chancellor was lonely.

Chapter 12

Feu de Joie

Defutois entered the music room filled with confidence. Quantz had carefully instructed him on the proper and accepted etiquette in the presence of royalty. "The formalities of stance and the intimations of gesture are as vital as the definitions of words," Quantz had decreed. He had overheard other courtiers claim that the King wished to dispense with dull ceremony for the more informal manners of republican etiquette. He had also noticed that Baron Belfort affected an air of casualness with the King, so Defutois assumed a relaxed posture. He decided to follow Belfort's example and leave Quantz' advice for more ceremonial occasions. He turned his back on the King with an air of studied nonchalance before bending into his bow.

When he rose, Frederick's eyes bored outrage into him. Disconcerted by the royal glare, he attempted to placate the stare. "I hope Your Majesty is in excellent health as always." Frederick's jaw dropped in flabbergasted incredulity just enough to expose a row of rotten teeth.

"If I am always in excellent health, it is superfluous to ask the question," Frederick replied and beckoned Defutois with a menacing finger.

Defutois dutifully approached Frederick's chair and saw a piece of paper spread before him on the desk. He immediately recognized the sonnet he had corrected. Frederick cast a glower of contempt over Defutois' pencilled improvements. It was one thing to make a suggestion. It was quite another to discover mistakes. But it was something akin to treason to flaunt any error in Frederick's poetry.

Frederick stabbed his fingernail at the paper. "What is the meaning of this?" Defutois felt a tremor run from his fingers to his chest as he looked at his own corrections of Frederick's sentences. "Oh," Defutois exclaimed, "that is the verb 'parteger'. Its primary meaning, it is 'to share'."

"I know what the word means, you dolt. I want to know why you have changed the spelling."

Defutois dredged up his last remaining reserves of aplomb, but his voice rattled with uncertainty. "It is more of an improvement and a suggestion than a criticism, Your Majesty."

Frederick looked into the distance and his eyes followed the silver tracery from the wall to the ceiling. His aloof and concentrated attention to every detail of the decoration implied that the very sight of Defutois was both odious to his person and an assault upon his taste.

"Your suggestion is to substitute my 'partagerons', for 'we share' to 'partagerai' because 'I share'," he said with studied contempt.

"The change will help the meter of the line," Defutois attempted to explain. He judged that honesty would be the best and safest policy. "The beauty of the line must correspond to the word."

Frederick snapped his head back to the paper, paused, and pointed to the word. "And you think 'I will share' is prettier than 'we will share'?" he quietly demanded.

"That would improve the poetry."

Defutois attempted to divert Frederick's attention to the text of his poem. He was hoping that a friendly disagreement on style would disarm Frederick's dangerous malice.

Frederick's response to the improvements proved to Defutois that he had made a disastrous error in judgment. The king turned his glowering hatred on Defutois. The fire in his eyes quenched any desire to please.

"And you are so ignorant that you do not know that 'we' is used for royal persons?"

Defutois persisted in his futile effort to lead him back to the poem and looked directly into Frederick's eyes. "But the poem is declaimed by a simple shepherd, so 'I' is more fitting to the scene and to the character."

Defutois cringed before those eyes filled with rage.

"How dare you look me in the eye," Frederick said so evenly that he was attempting to control his outrage at such an affront to his dignity.

Defutois clasped his mouth shut, but his ears blistered.

Frederick's eyes narrowed as his lips pursed. "I had wondered why they had sent me such an incompetent. Now I know. You are nothing but a dirty little spy. You come to my court pretending to assist my literary work and all the time you are sneaking around looking for information to bring back to your masters. You disgust me. You are no better than the French whores, wheedling for favors from the courtiers they pleasure."

Defutois was rendered mute before such raging accusations. All his stratagems to diffuse such anger were worse than useless, for they only fueled this storm of raging indignation. It was even too late to placate him with abject submission.

"Your stupid improvements have made me late for the review of my Guard. Get out," Frederick screamed.

Defutois ran from the room in panic. The only words he heard were "guard" and "out" and his fear gave wings to his feet. He imagined one of the king's hussars running down the corridor at the command "guard" and heard the scraping of a saber being unsheathed. He ran away from the apparition of the pursuing guard and found himself at the head of the stairs leading to the lower levels of the palace. If he had had the courage to look behind him, he would have seen that there was no burly henchman chasing him with a flashing blade. The predator was nothing more than the product of his terrified imagination. He knew it was the staircase Heinz had used to lead them out of the palace after their little escapade with the Shepherdess. His feet straggled as quickly as they could carry him from step-to-step and he reached the bottom without tumbling.

He heard voices beyond a door, flung it open, and careened into a room filled with a cloud of steam. He bumped into bare breasted women sloshing buckets of hot water over the pots they were scouring. The sudden appearance of a gentleman dressed in a fine coat set them all shrieking in laughter and their taunts filled the scullery.

Defutois was brought to a sudden and flustered stop by the sight of so many sweat lathered breasts shaking with screams of frolicking derision. One threw a soap sodden rag at him and he thundered into a run before the whole pack of harridans attacked. He dashed through the greasy cloud and the cruel gibes to the far door, running the gauntlet of ecstatic women eager for a little sport in the midst of their tedious labors.

Defutois reached the path behind the palace and grappled at a tree trunk to regain his breath. He felt the sapling sway under his weight but was desperate to escape. In a few moments, he saw this was the place where Heinz had led them on their adventure, but without his guide, he was completely lost. In his confusion, he could not remember which direction led out of the palace, but his indecision afforded the chance to breathe deeply and control his raging heart.

He ran to the right, seeking the comforting sounds of the stable, but only the branches of the orange trees greeted his search. There was no welcoming ringing of anvils, no comforting clinking of harnesses to reveal his position. He sniffed for the reassurance of horse dung, but could only smell rotten oranges. The silence was as threatening as Frederick's shouting, but he kept walking in the hope he would find a gate.

Terror clouded his mind, so he never realized that his feet were stepping up the hill. The gates were all at the bottom of the palace mound, but he could not remember the way out. He trudged along the path until he saw a group of servants walking ahead of him. They must be going somewhere that did not lead back to the King and he judged he would be safer if he looked like he was one of them. His coat was finer than their clothing, but if he stepped back, nobody would take a second look at his uniform. He followed them to the buildings of the Chancery behind the palace. They mounted the stairs to the terrace, and this gave him the chance to orient himself. The terrace thronged with all ranks of the palace servants.

The crowd had a holiday atmosphere and lined the terrace railings overlooking the parade ground of the palace guard. Defutois skulked at the edge of the crowd, hoping their numbers would disguise his presence. He was shaking and tried to gain enough control of himself to remain inconspicuous. He looked back along the path, but no hussar appeared with the gleaming blade to slice his flesh. Either he had evaded his pursuer or the King's sentry had not existed at all. He felt a little ashamed that he might have imagined the guard, but convinced himself that in such a dreadful situation it was better to run from an illusion than to remain waiting for an actual threat. Now that he had no fear of his immediate execution, a worse horror crept into his mind. After such a scene, he had no future. His prospects of any favor evaporated under Frederick's rage. It was his first and last glimpse of the madness that sits upon a throne.

His nerves jolted when he felt something pulling the tails of his coat. He turned expecting to see the hussar materialize, but Heinz' voice was at the other end of the tug. "You will enjoy this," Heinz assured him.

"Enjoy what?" Defutois bleated.

"It will be a fudejwa," Heinz informed him.

Defutois head quivered in fearful incomprehension, but in its shaking he saw Stephan leaning over the balustrade and gazing at the lines of the Royal Guard formed into a square on the parade ground. Stephan turned to see where Heinz had disappeared and when he spied Defutois, beckoned the Frenchman with a wave of invitation. Defutois' relief prodded him to follow Heinz, pushing the servants aside and clearing a path through the grumbling crowd to join Stephan.

Stephan eyed Defutois' rib-shackled breathing and said, "You have been exercising?"

"I have had a shock," Defutois confessed, and quickly avoided any further explanation, "in the scullery."

Stephan laughed at the thought and assured Defutois, "Those hags are very comfortable but they would also tear you to pieces. You were lucky to escape their unnatural appetites."

Heinz' face flashed agreement with Stephan's warning, but also with a hint of fond pleasures.

"But what is this?" Defutois pleaded. "I could only get some jumbled words out of Heinz."

Stephan swept his arm over the parade ground and said, "This is a royal Feu de Joie."

"I heard a most disconcerting 'fudejwa' and had no idea what he was talking about."

"Now that you have the French, you will witness your first German 'fire of joy'. It is really quite impressive, if you like the loud banging of five hundred muskets."

"There will be shooting?"

144

"It is a celebration and a salute from the Royal Guard to His Majesty."

"What are they celebrating?" Defutois inquired with feigned interest.

"Who knows?" Stephan responded with his habitual shrug. "I could not care less if they will fire their guns to announce that His Majesty has been delivered of a stinking and fetid stool."

Defutois smirked to think of these lines of soldiers standing to rigid attention for a chamber pot. "So, it is a parade," he said.

"They will march around and form a line before the King. The Giants all stand before him and raise their muskets. They all shoot into the air in a rapid succession as a salute."

Heinz was quick to add, "They call it a 'running fire of guns'."

Defutois looked over Stephan's shoulder but was careful to remain hidden. He watched Frederick slowly ride his horse to the edge of the parade ground, turn to face the rows of Giants. Defutois was glad to look at the horse's backside, for it meant that Frederick would not spot him in the crowd.

They listened to orders shouted within the ranks of guardsmen and the files all rotated like doors closing together to form one long line before the King. Frederick raised his hat and bowed in gracious acknowledgement of the precision of their maneuver and every voice shouted "hurrah" together in grateful thanks for His Majesty's praise. Defutois felt the thunderous bellow hit him like a hot wave. Their united roar merged into a wave that echoed in repeated peals off the Chancery wall behind him.

Before the sound had dissipated, every Giant raised his musket to his shoulder and took aim at the sky. Frederick sat calmly waiting their volley of acclamation. From the far left of the line, each soldier fired his weapon in a rapid sequence so that the whole line cascaded in puffs of flaming powder in just a few seconds. The discipline required for this display of concentration before the King was impressive even to Defutois' eyes filled with suspicions of danger.

They heard a shriek from the line of Giants. Every eye turned to see one soldier's musket clatter to the ground. Before he could replace his hat, Frederick glowered at the screaming soldier who had dared to fall out of line.

Defutois saw the soldier's head smoldering. When the Giant had raised his musket, it had slipped in his sweaty palms, and the muzzle flare had set fire to his wig. The heavily powdered and greased plaits had burst into flame under his hat, and the Giant was desperately trying to pull it off. He broke ranks and ran past Frederick towards the lawn just under the terrace. Frederick exploded in laughter to see one of his Giants cavorting with his head on fire. The audience on the terrace joined in with the general merriment and howled at the unexpected comedy.

The soldier threw himself on the grass and struggled on his knees to pull off his hat and wig. Heinz pointed a finger, and Stephan and Defutois saw that the soldier was Gregori. Some men, lounging on the steps, ran to him taking off their coats to smother the flames. Before they could reach him, the fire slithered from his head and caught on his cross-belts that gleamed with the pitch he had used to clean them. The flames snaked down over his shoulders and bisected his body until they found a refuge in his cartridge pouch. The pouch contained the regulation twenty little parcels of power and shot. The laughter ceased as abruptly as the explosion engulphed Gregori.

The man was a shuddering scream. The bullets had all exploded in a chain of deadly missiles and tore him from hip to chest. The poor man was instantly half butchered but still alive.

The terrace was in rigid shock. Stephan was too late to shield Heinz' eyes from the conflagration and the boy gaped into the bloody cavern that had become the poor man's chest. All could see his heart beating to the open sky.

Defutois could not pull his eyes from the scene but his ears heard the royal command to "Marche." A glance told him that Frederick had commanded the regiment to continue with the parade. Every soldier's face was stone as they reformed their lines and marched to the tune of The King's March. The regimental band led the jaunty procession away, following Frederick's horse prancing sedately to the rhythm of the anthem.

Servants ran to the soldier's aid. They were oblivious to the danger of more bullets joining the fusillade and stamped out the flames. Gregori convulsed with pain and the realization that he would not have very long to live. Defutois heard the cry of "Get a priest" ripple along the terrace and knew there was only one end to this horror.

The screams had sunk to a low moaning, barely audible over the sprightly marching of the martial music. The thousand feet of the Royal Guard smothered the soldier's last gasps of life and Defutois saw Frederick's horse fade into the distance at the head of the columns, as if what had occurred was nothing more than a minor intrusion upon his parade. Frederick was so clearly unmoved by the soldier's demise, that Defutois's fear of retribution evaporated under his utter revulsion.

He grasped the stone railing with both hands but he had not the strength to support himself. Stephan turned to see Defutois slide to the ground and caught him before his head went crashing into the stone. Heinz helped Stephan lay Defutois gently down, and they knew something was dreadfully wrong with the Frenchman.

Curious servants circled the trio, but Stephan commanded them to stand back. He pulled Defutois' coat, scattering silver buttons at their feet. One servant girl quickly stepped on a button, and casually bent over to pick it up. She wondered why he was in such a state. Stephan pulled off the cravat strangling Defutois, and Heinz pulled back the wig. Defutois eyes fluttered erratically, but he was breathing, so Stephan nodded to Heinz to pick him up.

Stephan raised Defutois by the shoulders and Heinz threw the legs under his arms. They formed a little procession along the terrace, followed by a double file of curious servants eager to find out what had happened. They carried Defutois' gasping but limp body to the end of the terrace and disappeared down the stairs.

The servants returned to the spectacle of the King's review of his guard.

The Memoir of Charles Defutois

Part the Fourth

Paris, Lazarette Prison,

July 27, 1794

I sit waiting for the morning to thaw my bones and my memory. I can sit because the kindly guard appeared with a chair. This must be one of Paul's gifts. He has his way of dealing with my guards and it makes me proud he is my son.

Paul laughed when he told me that some can be bought, others submit to his rank, and the rest fear his threats. I do not doubt him. His lips are formed for promise, for superiority, and for violence. The father is worthy of such a good son.

The guard who brought the chair has none of the bullying swagger of the others. His quietude is comforting, when it is not terrifying. The man is illiterate and only the crevices of toil upon his face tell of his age.

When he deposited the chair, he carefully placed it where our nods and fingers pointed. The chair's legs did not scrape the stone floor, for the man was very careful not to damage a thing of such obvious value. This was done not as the deference of the peasant. His motions were considerate of my desires for he wished to please me.

He had looked over each shoulder before pulling a coin from his pocket and holding it close my face. He had whispered, "The man. Your son," and clenched his fist around the talisman he cherished more as a gift rather than as a bribe.

I am sure he has never been acquainted with gentlemen. He calls me "M'sieur" and lisps through the passages of absent teeth. His "M'sieur" is so much more comforting than the three hammer blows of "Citoyen" shouted as a last command.

Yesterday, the guards herded the rest of the prisoners into the last parade. They had chalked numbers on the cell doors so each could take their rightful place in the procession. I heard no "M'sieur" when an old rag wiped the number from my door.

I have learned the patience of the listener. I accept every noise as a recital bearing tales of despair but also of hope. Any empty prison is a most fearful place. Vacant cells still hold the whispers. A profound and lifeless silence drips like dying icicles. It is then when the terror fills my skull like high tide flooding a cave. I sit waiting for the pain to ebb and finish its terrible recessional.

The sun has cast my grid upon the floor. It is with some relief that I see only the last row remains. The pictures have told me too many stories to be a comfort. Such tales bring as much accusation as relief but I must listen to what they say. I regret nothing. I would not change much for we are impotent to cast a net into our futures.

Some whine "if only" they had taken the other path. They believe they would not have arrived. "If only" they whimper through useless lamentations of what might have been and curse themselves for their foolish choices. As if they could. What would have changed? "If only" they believe their choice was but two paths. At each turning there were hundreds of routes all diverging through life only to meet at the end. Why burden yourself with such a tangled web?

Now I have but few pictures. The chapters are meagre fare. I have chosen to enjoy them and to listen to whatever they have to tell me. Those little events remain and I am curious to see what I have become.

Chapter 13

Sanctuary

Quantz was enjoying his walk home from the Chancery. The sunset mellowed the strangely vacant streets. All the people had deserted the town to watch the King review his guard, so nobody blocked his path.

He had often noted that the parades were more popular than the concerts and the operas, or for that matter, any other public performance. One sat reverently at the opera in dutiful appreciation of the King's largesse in offering such an expensive entertainment. But it was like being caged in church and scourged by a preacher ranting in French or Italian or in any other garble the people did not understand.

But the parades were all in German. The commands were easy to follow, no matter how guttural, for the sergeants' throaty voices could be heard above the cheering crowds. The people felt they were part of the parade and so every maneuver filled them with pride, for these marching ranks were filled with many of their own.

He slowed to hear the distant thunder from the palace and relished the noise diminishing behind him. Anna would be overjoyed by his news. What with Stephan and Heinz now permanent guests, the house's walls seemed to shrink under the burden of all these people. Still, he looked forward to Anna's joy when he announced that they would be getting another room. He would have it constructed from the kitchen to the back garden. With a little prodding, he knew he could get the masons to "throw in a few more bricks" and expand their home beyond Potsdam's regimented dimensions. Only a few extra feet that the inspectors would not notice and his workshop would bloom into whatever Anna wanted it to be.

He passed the shuttered windows of the baker and the blacksmith, for they had declared a holiday and left their trade deserted. Under the linden tree before his door, he stopped to look up at the two stories that were his house. He was proud that his skills and his talents had been made manifest in actual bricks and mortar. There were many musicians who lived as vagabonds from court to court, making money, but always traveling. Such people lived in coaches that soon grew wearisome and risked getting more fleas in their wigs from the stinking beds of wayside inns. To be settled and secure was worth all his effort.

The windows gleamed under Anna's careful scouring and he was thankful that he never had to concern himself with the domestic squalor that was the habitation of the unmarried musician. When he visited the abodes of other members of the royal band, he almost gagged from the stench of unwashed feet and soiled linen. They were oblivious to the dirt in which they lived and kept the filth at bay with another bottle of perfume. He mused that his house had magically appeared out of his flute, which was quite true. Anna had given him so much. She had made their house a refuge from the threatening graciousness of the court. The palace was a place to act the part he had made for himself. There was profit in his performance. But the house was his place of utter safety. When Anna would fall into one her bad tempers, he would remind himself of the stink of bachelors and wait for her storms to subside. Now it was his happy duty to return her favors.

The last of the day warmed his back as he trod with joyous steps and happier thoughts to his front door. He swung the door open to be greeted by Defutois' drunken ravings.

"I have no idea what was the problem," Defutois cried.

Anna sat beside him at the table unable to comfort him in her confusion. Stephan looked more serious in his brooding than Quantz had ever seen. Heinz stood apart, perplexed but also curious by all the commotion surrounding him. Anna turned to her husband standing in the door frame and her eyes were full of desperate need. "What has happened?" Quantz demanded.

His attitude, more commanding than annoyed, gave Anna relief. It was his way of making a demand for facts and an appeal to reason. She was quick to answer, "Stephan and Heinz brought him here. He had some sort of fit."

"But what happened?" Quantz repeated, with growing irritation.

"He collapsed during the parade," Stephan recounted.

"What was the Frenchman doing in the parade?"

"We were on the Chancery terrace when it happened."

"We saw the whole thing," Heinz added, brooding over the sight gouged into his memory.

"What whole thing?" Quantz demanded. "The parade?"

"You don't know the news?" Anna asked.

"What news? I have been with the Chancellor," Quantz explained. He controlled his growing temper and turned to Stephan. "You are unclear. Again, what happened?"

"He blew up," Heinz said.

"Defutois?"

"No. Gregori."

"Gregori who?" Quantz asked.

"Gregori, the Giant."

Defutois saw Quantz through his cloud of brandy and wheedled, "I had no idea he would blow up."

Anna saw that Quantz's patience was near its end and offered a seat. Quantz sat and she calmly informed him. "A bad thing happened during the parade."

Quantz was getting the impression that somehow Defutois was responsible for something that had happened to this giant, Gregori, but was no nearer a clear account of this obviously terrible event, whatever it was. Quantz gathered all of his self-control to ward off the chaos of their tale and asked gently of Stephan, "You were there?"

"Yes, and I wish I had not witnessed such a scene," Stephan confessed.

"Tell me," Quantz coaxed.

Stephan took a swig of brandy from the glass before him and acknowledged Anna's nod of permission to continue. Quantz sat dumbfounded at the account of Gregori's death. He could picture the place, the time, the people for he had been made to suffer through many of the regimental exercises that were an assault upon his eyes and his ears.

He knew that nothing would ever be allowed to intrude on Frederick's reviews of his personal guard regiment, so the flaming demise of one soldier was nothing more than an intrusion upon the performance of their duties. He had ignored tens of thousands of such corpses on dozens of fields of battle. Dying on the parade ground was just bad manners.

When Stephan recounted the collapse of Defutois, Quantz understood how witnessing such a dreadful scene would affect a young man. Gregori's death was horrific enough, but Quantz sensed there was something else he needed to know. The bare facts insinuated a threat. Defutois was maudlin drunk, so Quantz played along with the Frenchman's sorrows.

"But you were perfectly hale when I last saw you at the door of the music room."

"Then it all went wrong," Defutois whined.

"You broke the door?"

"No. All I was doing was correcting his grammar."

"Gregori's grammar?"

"No. The King's poem."

"What poem?"

"Some nonsense about a shepherd," Defutois complained. "It was really bad."

"The shepherd?"

"No. The poem. I corrected the grammar and he raged at me for doing what he told me to do."

"Yes. It is so unfair."

Defutois lurched at them over the table. "I'll tell you a secret." He wagged a conspiratorial finger in their faces and exclaimed, "He writes shit."

Quantz was painfully acquiring some of the details of an incident involving some clash of poetics between Frederick and Defutois. What little he could gather from Defutois' simpering suggested something more than a gentleman's disagreement as to style.

"A child could make better allusions to the wonders of the classics," Defutois lectured. "I really don't know why I bother."

Quantz was almost fearful to continue, but he had to know. Danger lurked in the fumes of Defutois breath.

"So what happened when you corrected the poem's grammar?"

"I looked him square in the eyes and told him that the personal pronoun should be singular and not plural and he just went insane."

"You looked into the King's eyes?" Anna inquired, incredulously.

Stephan and Quantz exchanged knowing glances, until Defutois wailed, "I don't understand."

"No one is allowed to look directly into the King's eyes." Anna explained with sudden and terrifying understanding.

"But I saw you do it," Defutois accused Quantz. "So I did what you did."

"Nobody other than Quantz may look into the King's eyes," Stephan reiterated with a heat that brought Defutois out of his stupor.

"But I just did as you did," Defutois wheedled.

The enormity of the situation jumped at them. Quantz could appreciate the appalling implications and imagine the immediate danger to them all. They were mired in the facts of Gregori and Defutois. They could not see the threat to themselves.

Defutois' emotions welled into desperation, as the brandy coursed through him. Quantz saw the feeling was self-pity in the face of disaster. Defutois cast his head into his hands splayed over the table and Anna wrapped an arm around his shuddering shoulders. Quantz looked at this tableau of disaster and his mind reeled with the possibilities. Stephan looked lost. Quantz saw that only Heinz appeared calm, almost resigned. "Heinz. Take him upstairs." Heinz rose quickly and pulled Defutois' arm around his neck. He lifted the sobbing man and walked him to the stairs with surprising expertise. Quantz waited until the footsteps draggled over the upper floor and Defutois' weeping was a distant mist.

"Well, this is bizarre," Quantz exclaimed.

"What are we to do?" Anna asked, submissive in her ignorance.

"First we find out all we can about the cause of this display." Quantz demanded.

Stephan searched for answers to questions he had barely formulated, and Quantz saw that he was stumped.

"Why didn't you leave him at his quarters?" Quantz asked.

"We didn't know what had happened. He had some sort of fit, so we thought you would be able to call a doctor."

"He may need a doctor in the morning, but there is no medicine for this disease."

"You think he is that sick?" Anna inquired with mounting apprehension.

"We must be careful that we are not infected," Quantz said.

"Could it be a plague?" Stephan shuddered.

Quantz sat back with his hands behind his head, more to reassure the others than to relieve the tension blossoming in his head. "I meant the worse plague. He has displeased the King. We know only the barest pieces of information as to the cause, but we know the result if he is caught in this house."

Anna sucked in air. Stephan groaned his agitation and offered the feeblest of excuses, "I never thought of that."

"Now is the time when we should be thinking of this," Quantz mused aloud. "If the guards find him here, we will bear the brunt of the anger. The Frenchman can be dismissed and sent home to France. Where will we go if we share his fate?"

They heard Heinz' feet apologetically squeaking down the stairs. When he appeared, Quantz' finger beckoned him and he demanded the boy's full attention.

"You are to go to Defutois' house. Collect his clothes and bring them back here."

Heinz neither bowed nor scraped but stood proud to receive his commission, He assented with a simple, "Yes" and left the house with a steady tread.

"Can we trust him?" Stephan mused with growing apprehension.

"We must," Quantz stated the obvious and Anna knew her husband was teasing out a simple solution to a most complex and frightening problem.

"What shall we do with him?" she asked.

"We'll keep him here until a more permanent solution presents itself."

They sat in the midst of their uncertainty. The slightest gossip would have the guards at the door and they would all be kicked out. There would be no ceremony and no explanation. Defutois had kindled Frederick's ire and anybody who gave sanctuary to the criminal would suffer along with the condemned. Offering any aid to the sinner would make them complicit in his sin. The moment Defutois was returned to Frederick's clutches would be the ruin of them all.

Quantz' heart went out to Anna. He could see the fear flashing in her eyes. They were becoming moist with anxiety, so he touched her hand and whispered, "It will all be resolved."

"But how?" she begged.

"To our advantage," he said.

Anna took renewed courage from her husband's assurance. He had a way of making things come out well. When she was most worried about the future, he would smile and say, "Something would turn up when we least expect it and least recognize good fortune leering into our very faces."

Most often, she was confused by the seemingly senseless actions of those around her, but Quantz could see the patterns which evaded her. She told herself that it was because of the music that he had this strange talent to find order in confusion. Maybe the music had taught him that there were causes and effects unknown to her but clear to him. He had his ways and it was to wait on circumstances and search for the answer to the riddle. Whatever was the source of his alchemy, she knew she had to trust it now. There was no time to quibble or to blame. They could not sit waiting for the retribution of shame. There was just too much at stake for her to berate the man who would lead them through this trial. Her hand returned the tenderness of his touch and she confessed with all the courage she could muster, "I know."

Heinz slowly opened the door and entered with a large bundle slung over his shoulder. Anna quickly withdrew her hand from Quantz' grasp and rose to greet the boy. "What have we here?" she asked. Heinz dropped the bundle to the floor with a muffled thud. He flung back the corners of the blanket he had used to retrieve Defutois' clothes.

"I only brought his clothes," Heinz said.

"What else was left?" Anna asked.

"There were two trunks full of books but I thought he'd need his pants and coats more than some useless old books. Besides, they were too heavy to carry."

"You did right," Quantz praised.

Heinz stood to the side to allow Anna to examine the haul. She pulled out garments as if she were sorting them for the laundry tub. "Three pairs of pants," she counted, "five shirts." Heinz looked at a white tangle of soiled hosiery and Anna declared, "Stockings and socks fit for the tub."

Stephan and Quantz smiled to see Anna throw herself into the task of laundering Defutois' clothes. His very presence signaled catastrophe, but Anna was busy solving their most immediate problem. It was so like her, Quantz thought. She would change what she could and leave the impossible to sort itself out. Quantz watched her bent over the pile and accepted the glaring truth that he would have to deal with the impossible.

Stephan looked over the clothing scattered over the floor. "No shoes?"

"I didn't see any," Heinz confessed sheepishly. Stephan's eyes lowered to Heinz' feet to see if he had purloined any of Defutois' footwear. Heinz's shoes had the same tell-tale scuffs and gouges he had seen in the workshop, and was relieved that Heinz was neither a thief nor a liar.

"He won't need shoes for a while," Quantz added.

"Why?" Stephan begged,

"Because he won't be going anywhere."

"He is to remain your prisoner?" Stephan asked.

"We must get him out of the house," Anna simply stated

"We must get him out of Prussia." Quantz proclaimed.

The first scent of a plan was forming itself in Quantz' mind but it was as vague and tantalizing as snatches of music played by the wind. He could hear something calling but dare not follow until the vision was just a little more formed. He had learned as a young man that chimeras are always dangerous. A temptation at this stage would be lethal. Obeying the first solution to such a problem would be just a step to a disaster beyond their comprehension, so he ignored the desire to work fast. Whatever would happen, would be at a slow enough tempo for him to control.

He left them searching through Defutois' worldly possessions and walked to the window. The street was a silent reply to his yearning for clarity. Over his shoulder he asked, "Did anyone see you bringing Defutois here?"

Heinz as casually answered, "Everybody was at the parade."

A simple fact could form the frame of a plan. As far as he could gather, Defutois' presence in the house was their secret. Therefore, the secrecy must be maintained until the solution presented itself.

He looked through the window at the blinking sky. The stars cast waves of colored light over the whole town. He could hear revelry from distant houses, but he blocked his ears to the distraction. He could faintly hear the stars twinkle, for the night was so much clearer than his mind. He envied the adamant simplicity of night. All was suppressed in darkness and that was where he saw the most light.

He begged the night to reveal their very uncertain future. Always, when there was some decision to be made, he felt as though he were falling through a torn net. So much of his life had been a jarring change ushered in by some uninvited visitor.

He had been a boy holding tongs for the village blacksmith when the priest had arrived with the news that he was now an orphan. The death of his mother was as sudden as the passing of his father had been quick. Both left him bereft of the closeness other children took for granted. The adults gathered in the house and he had been ordered to wait outside. Barred from their presence, he had listened at the window to their deliberations. There had been hurried whispers played to a counterpoint of adamant assertions and he had been vaguely aware that he was the subject of their discussions.

When they recalled him to announce his future, he was shocked to be informed that he was to live with a distant uncle and become a musician. All he had ever known of music was the rhythms of the anvil and now he was to take in his hands pieces of wood and make them sing. It was all so ridiculous, all so unimagined. They had put together his bundle of clothes, much smaller than the one cluttering his floor now and sent him on his way. For all he knew, he had been in the same situation as Defutois but in a village, not a king's palace.

The deaths had been so quiet. They were a mere rattling in the throat followed by the silence that would never break. Now there was the need for a silence that would help them to live. If that silence were broken, so would they be.

The window grew cold with his thought, so he thrust his hand into his pocket searching for warmth. His fingers felt the parts of his flute that he habitually carried in his coat, and the night spoke. As his salvation came with the strange instruments his uncle had cast to him, so too the answer to their riddle was at his very finger tips.

Chapter 14

Whispering Walls

Anna's joints protested as she forced herself to prepare breakfast. She had called up the stairs for the others to "Hurry" and Quantz and Defutois stood suspended halfway down. Stephan and Heinz stood in the kitchen, hungry and eager to obey her insistent invitation.

The front door shook with three resounding thumps. They froze and Quantz' scowl commanded Defutois to get back to the bedroom. Defutois hurriedly obeyed to the accompaniment of three more knocks of greater insistence. Quantz motioned for Anna to answer the summons and she walked down the corridor to the door. Breathing deeply, she wore her most annoyed face as she turned the handle and flung open the door.

A troop of workmen stood at the entrance and pulled off their hats for the lady confronting them. Anna hid her relief that they were not the palace guards searching for the missing Frenchman and calmly bid them, "Good morning."

The man who seemed to be their leader responded with a polite "Good Morning, Mistress." Anna was still flustered by this visitation of dusty workmen and could only say, "Yes. The morning is very good. Nice morning air. But who are you?" The man assured her, "I am Hans." Anna had to ask, "And what do you want?" The men all laughed at her discomfort until Hans clarified, "We want to make some walls."

They could almost hear a sigh of relief from the whole house and Quantz mastered his anxiety to descend the stairs and approach them. He spoke directly to Hans but his voice wrapped around them all. "I take it that you are the bricklayers." They all puffed up at the recognition and Hans assured him, "Not just the bricklayers. We're the best bricklayers in all of Potsdam." A taller man added, "All of Berlin." The gang of five burst into a chorus, "All of Prussia," and laughed aloud in exaggerated self mockery at their anthem to their abilities.

When Quantz observed them armed with trowels and not swords, he enjoyed their comradely bragging. "We can't allow the best bricklayers in all of Prussia to stand in the street," and bid them, "Please, enter."

The five trooped through the door and along the corridor to the kitchen leaving a trail of muddy footprints behind them. Stephan and Heinz stood to greet them and Quantz and Anna joined the throng. Hans cast a professional eye over the crowded kitchen and exclaimed, "It's a bit tight in here?"

Quantz agreed heartily and showed Hans the back door to the garden. Hans leaned on the door jamb and looked into the area immediately behind the kitchen. "No problem," he pronounced. Quantz gathered the rough quintet before him and asked, "Is there anything I can get you?" Five heads nodded and shouted together, "Beer." Quantz turned with a smile to Anna and said, "You heard them." Anna called "Heinz" and the boy jumped to her command. "Go to the baker. Bring back what the men need."

The masons laughed in their knowledge of working for a kindly customer. Hans stepped through the back door. He paced the yard and rubbed his chin philosophically. Quantz was intrigued by the man's poses and followed him around the area that soon would be transformed into another room. Hans stood in the center of the door opening and raised his right hand level with the ground. Gunther chalked a mark on the wall behind Hans where his fingertips indicated. Hans repositioned himself with his back to the chalk mark. Quantz watched this strange ballet and followed Hans' arm until there were five evenly spaced chalk marks slashed on the wall. "There," Hans assured him. The new wall will start here," and he drew an upright arrow over the bricks.

Quantz' eye gauged the final dimensions and said to Hans, "Won't it be a little small for a workshop?"

"All the rooms in Potsdam must be ten arm lengths in size. It's the rule and we must obey the rules."

Quantz looked disappointed and Hans was enjoying the master's chagrin. When he judged he had tormented Quantz enough, he ordered, "Gunther," and the taller man stood in the doorway.

"I have to check my measurements, so do it again." Gunther grinned with the knowledge of one who had performed this charade many times before and raised his arm. Hans made another chalk mark and repeated the process. Quantz watched the lanky Gunther dutifully raise his arm and waddle to the left. When Gunther's arm descended after the fifth chalk mark, Quantz saw they had considerably increased the future room's dimensions.

Hans turned in satisfaction to Quantz and said, "The rules say five arm lengths. They say nothing about whose arm." Quantz and the masons shared in the general glee and Quantz laughed in the satisfaction that these men could obey in the most defiant manner. They would do an excellent job.

Heinz reappeared and asked for help with a barrel. The word immediately got their attention and the masons all rushed through the house to the front door. They gathered around a wheelbarrow loaded with a huge beer barrel and manhandled their precious cargo back through the house to their work area. Anna followed, shouldering a satchel of bread loaves and five tankards. They quickly helped her with her burden and pounced on the keg with shouts of "Good Beer" and "Buns" and toasted the Quantz family with their frothy breakfast.

Gunther looked up to see Defutois' face disappear from the window above his head. It was none of his business how many people lived in the Quantz house, but he concluded that, when they had finished their work, Quantz would be able to make some extra money renting out rooms His more pressing need was to get as much beer as possible into his stomach in the shortest time. His four companions followed his example and Quantz knew they would not start work until they were fully and fluidly prepared. "We will need another barrel," he whispered to Anna. "At least," she replied.

Many tankards later, they were drunk enough to begin their labors. Hans inquired as to the purpose of the projected room and at the news it was to be a workshop, said, "In that case we'll do you a double." Quantz had no idea what a double was, but surrendered to Hans' knowledge and authority. "Rakes," Hans ordered and they all trooped through the house.

Stephan and Anna stood on the pavement and watched them scamper over a wagon piled full of bricks. They retrieved shovels and rakes from the wagon's bed and marched feet through the house to the yard.

The wagon was so overloaded that the solitary horse pulling it slumped its head in bewildered exhaustion. Anna watched the poor creature stand shivering in patient resignation, its front leg bent in fatigue. She found a bucket hanging from the wagon's staves, filled it at the street pump, and returned to the horse. When she went to pat the grizzled muzzle, her hand recoiled from the heat rising from the beast's head. The eyes blinked in slow supplication and Anna slowly poured the water over the matted mane. She repeated her journey to the pump and back, until she heard the snorts give way to wheezy sighs. The horse dipped its lips into the pool welling on the cobblestones and slurped in satisfaction. When the horse shook its head in delight, Anna knew the animal was safe. She decided to stay in the kitchen and make sandwiches.

She gathered the loaves and sliced five of them through the middle. A quick look into the larder and she found enough cheese to make a substantial meal whenever they needed it. She knew that it was best to be prepared and that any work was quicker on a satisfied stomach. The results were always proportional to the quality of the food.

Quantz was happy to lean against the barrel and enjoy the performance. Hans lined up the other four at the house wall and raised his arms to conduct. "One" he bellowed and the line of rakes pulled back two feet in harmony. "Two" brought a repeat of the action and "Three" left a clear and even path before the retreating men. Hans made them rest while he inspected their work and when he judged that the ground was not level to his satisfaction, commanded them to return to the wall. All four took their places for this minuet of manual labor and danced to Hans' call until he was satisfied with their efforts. When they lined up again, Hans guided them further back into the yard until a completely flat rectangle emerged from the bumps and furrows of the ground. Quantz could see that Hans left no stone unturned. The area was bounded by the chalk marks left by Gunther's long arms on the wall.

It was so simple, but this sort of work could only be done by practiced hands working together. He mused that Hans and the workmen were simply following the same pattern as any orchestra. They needed neither baton nor whip to do their work. Despite the huge quantities of beer they had consumed, there were no staggering steps to ruin their handiwork. They must have done this hundreds of times to acquire such expertise, for their every movement was as definite as any musician and they deserved to be called virtuosi of the rake. They would never receive ovations for their labors but every foot that would eventually walk in their room would be silent praise to accomplished and completely forgotten talent.

When they were satisfied with their raking, they formed a line from the yard, through the house, to the pump in the street. They drew five buckets of water and reformed their line in the yard. Each man held a bucket in his left hand and at Hans' commands their right hands cast a palmful of water in a wide arc. Quantz thought they looked like sowers spreading seed at planting time. Where they had marched with their rakes, they now tiptoed with the water. Quantz observed that they left a fine and moist film as they stepped backwards to the house. The sprinkle was even and the dusty surface was flattened into a firm table of earth.

When they finished their watering, they all rose, stretched, and Hans assured Quantz that, "This is thirsty work." Quantz responded to the hint by offering his tankard and his arm invited them to the barrel. They all shuffled to the spout and rose their tankards in foaming salute "to the Quantz family." Anna knew that the toasts would continue until the barrel was empty so she set her sandwiches on the kitchen table.

Anna hoped they would enjoy the feast and retreated to the dining room to give them privacy, but stayed close enough to hear their conversation. The men needed no prodding to settle on the kitchen floor with fistfuls of bread and cheese and the tankards poised to wash down their lunch.

"Your wife makes a great meal," Hans complimented Quantz on his luck and excellent choice in women.

"Very tasty," Gunther said.

"I won't need anything tonight," Bruno added.

Quantz nodded to Otto, the shortest of their company, and invited him into the conversation with a question. "Do they not feed you when you work?"

"Most people just want the job done," Herman grumbled sourly.

"We may as well be invisible," Bruno complained.

Quantz caught the resentment in his voice. "The worker deserves his fare in this house."

Hans laughed to hear Quantz proclaim the obvious fact that they were being treated well. They would return his consideration to the best of their abilities.

"It's good to keep your mouth shut and get the job finished," Otto declaimed.

"Like when you did that Valmore's wall," Hans added.

"That was some wall," and they shared a ribald laugh.

Quantz sensed they were dangling a veil over him and cocked his eyebrows in anticipation. "Valmore?" he asked.

"Madame Valmore," Hans returned with his eyebrows even higher in risqué suggestion.

"Was there something strange about that work?" Quantz asked.

"The strangest part was the Madame and the police," Hans teased.

"There was some fight involving this Madame?"

"No fight," Otto told him.

"Not a voice raised," Herman added.

"Bet there were lots of other things raised," Hans insinuated.

Hans knew he had caught Quantz' curiosity and launched into their oft repeated and always enjoyable story of the lady of their dreams.

"Madame Valmore is the most beautiful woman in Berlin," Hans avowed.

"Was the most beautiful lady in Berlin," Herman corrected.

"She died?"asked Quantz.

"She's deported," Herman clarified

"Back to France," Otto added and recalled with unrequited fantasy, "Out on her beautiful big ass."

"She had nipples like a cow," Herman dreamed.

Quantz listened with growing attention to their praises of the Madam's bulging and bovine charms. These men knew something that was tickling Quantz' memory and wrapped in the suspicion of a solution to his most pressing problem hiding upstairs.

"So what happened with this woman?" he asked.

Hans was quick to take the lead. "The policeman showed up and she was out within the hour."

"Out of her house?"

"Out of Berlin," Hans said.

"Where did she go?"

"Packed her off back to France."

"Without her furniture and clothes."

"They sent her away naked?" Quantz queried.

"With the clothes on her back."

"That would have been a sight worth seeing," Otto leered.

A strange scenario was emerging from their boisterous recollections and Quantz was careful not to delve too obviously. The slightest hint of betraying their confidences would render them mute.

"I wonder what she did for the police to take her away?" Quantz questioned.

"It was who she was doing." Hans added with authority and a hint of envy.

"The police?"

"There was just one policeman," Otto said.

"Tall man. Loads of medals on his chest," Herman added.

"Big wig," Hans scoffed. "Maybe you know who he is?"

"Sounds like Ramin," Quantz conjectured. "He's very important. He doesn't arrest people for being drunk in the streets."

"That's what we were thinking."

"Had to be really important."

"Ramin would not be doing this unless the King had ordered him." Quantz revealed.

They sobered quickly at the thought that whatever the Madame was up to had something to do with the barons and the palace. They were careful not to get too involved but were eager for Quantz to tell them all he could. Now that he had them in his grasp, he was happy to share what he knew.

"Ramin is the Governor of Berlin."

They all whistled at the rank of their gossip which only whetted their appetites for more.

"Ramin would only be used for the highest urgency, if he expelled this woman so quickly."

"It was quick but he was very polite," Otto added.

"Then that is truly Ramin. His manners are exquisite and his power absolute."

Otto and Herman were champing to relate all they had seen and heard while being ignored at the Madame's house. When he could no longer restrain himself, Herman blurted, "He gave her a bag and said that there were two hundred louis d'or and he even asked her to take it. Said if she took the bag, she would be doing him a favor."

"He wouldn't have to ask me twice," Hans confessed. "That's a pile of money."

"She complained that she had a lot of expensive furniture, Otto recalled. "and that man even told her that he would sell it at a price more than she could get and send her the money."

Clarity was emerging in Quantz' mind.

"She probably had the drip," Otto surmised.

"That's always the way with the French whores," Herman opined. "That's why I only go with our good German whores. No problems there."

Quantz knew it all. It was not just the trade of this woman but her origins. He remembered Frederick warning the orchestra of the dangers posed by the French courtesans. He claimed that, "German women pose little danger. The French women, who have infested Berlin, were different. They have a decided taste for intrigue."

The orchestra had dutifully listened to their king's injunctions as the masons were enthusiastically relating Madame Valmore's plight. Quantz recalled Frederick's proclamation, "The German women get all they can from their lovers but will not meddle in politics." For Frederick, this was the unforgivable sin. "When the French whores consort with my courtiers, they are more successful in their espionage." Frederick had railed again those French women, who knew neither their function nor their place. "They are paid twice," Frederick explained, "once by my court and the second time by the King of France for any information or influence they can acquire. I will have none of them in my territory. They are nothing but public plagues."

Now it was perfectly clear to Quantz. The expulsion of Madame Valmore was merely part of a general purge of the French women from Berlin. Frederick did not mind them plying their trade but he feared their pillow-talk. Many an army had been defeated in the boudoir before they arrived on the field of battle. It was the fact that she was French that was the problem. Defutois' insolence was bad enough but his nationality was a greater source of threat to Frederick. If Frederick was sweeping the French women out of his capital and the French tutor out of his study, then he was thinking about something French.

He sat back listening to their jokes about French tarts and said to himself, "Who says walls don't have ears? They also have voices. Even when those walls have not yet been raised."

Chapter 15

Minuet

Stephan stood waiting for the revelations of sunset. He had flung open all the doors and windows of the music room and invited the day's warmth to work its wonder. He leaned against the door frame opening onto the terrace and aimed his eyes at the floor. He and Heinz had set the last triangle in its place and the puzzle gleamed before them. The air almost bowed as it entered the room, sniffed approvingly through its circuit of the patchwork, and took its leave through the gaping windows with an approving sigh.

Early in the morning, they had waxed the whole surface for the last time. They had scrolled the thinest coating of the best wax over every inch of the floor. They had waxed themselves backwards to the terrace door and stood watching the moist veneer that must dry into a misty haze. Stephan's shoes now mounted guard on the terrace, where he had left them, so that he could walk in his stockings over the floor. His feet could not feel any variation where the sections joined and there was no snagging of his stockings by some errant splinter. He examined the misty swirls of wax filling every crevice from the door to each of the walls and knew his design was as intriguing as the veiled face of a beloved friend. "Yes," he exclaimed with satisfaction, "this is the best yet." He had created many rooms for royal feet, but this one would survive the ravages of time and the greater assaults of the many courtly hooves that would tread its surface. He explained to Heinz that, "Now we must just be patient."

They could only loiter while the wax dried under the sun's kindly alchemy. The door to the corridor had been locked so some rough-shod servant could not barge in and mar their handiwork. After three hours, Heinz was becoming restive. Stephan had learned that the boy combated his own boredom with a barrage of questions, so they had wiled away the time with Stephan's dissertations on sharpening a chisel.

It had taken some time for Stephan to trust Heinz with anything sharp, but the boy had persevered. After being instructed how to sharpen a saw with a file, Heinz had concentrated on acquiring the right angle to make the tiny teeth bite with a clean cut. The lessons had also produced so many cuts and scrapes on Heinz' fingers that Stephan came to the conclusion that the saw was trying to eat the boy. The first cut finger had produced laughter and the command, "Don't bleed on the wood."

Stephan had berated Heinz for ruining a perfectly cut piece and showed him that, no matter how hard he rubbed, the bloodstain would befoul the grain for all eternity. Heinz was almost in tears and bleated, "What do I do about it?" so Stephan picked up the bloody square and turned it up-side-down. The square fitted perfectly and nobody would ever see the imprint of Heinz' wound. When Heinz was reassured that his little accident would not destroy their work, Stephan turned his attention to the cut finger. With a dismissive grunt, Stephan had pulled a clove of garlic from his apron pocket. He slashed the clove and let the juice run into Heinz' lacerated finger. Heinz shuddered at the sharp jab but could see the blood staunch and feel the pain deaden. He obeyed Stephan's order to "hold the finger tightly," and when there was no longer any danger of defilement of their work or torment to Heinz' finger, they wrapped a strip of linen around the garlic coated finger and secured it with a bow neater than any lady's shoe lace.

Over the weeks, Heinz's fingers were festooned with so many bandages that his hands resembled a puppet show, but the boy cut through the pain and learned to accept the embarrassment. Stephan assured Heinz that these wounds would heel but their lessons would remain for the rest of his life. Gradually, the bandages disappeared and in their place Stephan acquired many perfectly cut squares, triangles, and lozenges. Heinz became so proficient with the saw, the chisel, and the plane that Stephan could concentrate on the composition of the floor without worrying that any piece would be out of joint.

Stephan had marveled that the boy was not only a quick learner but, with every skill he mastered, his curiosity increased. After cutting a perfectly straight tongue into one wooden triangle, he fitted it into the groove of a square and demanded to know why it was too tight. Stephan had initiated Heinz into the mysteries of humidity by pouring water over the join that had sparked Heinz' satisfaction with his workmanship. The wood rebelled at the water, swelled in outrage, and expanded until the tongue split and the two pieces collapsed. "There must be enough space for the wood to grow and then shrink when the temperature of the room changes." Heinz had looked over the half finished floor and asked, "Won't the whole floor come apart when the servants clean it?" Stephan laughed at the notion but appreciated the good sense of the question. "That's why we will cover everything with linseed oil and wax. The coating will seep between the pieces and soak the wood. When it dries, no water will get in." Instantly, Heinz understood that oil and wax would be used to clean such a floor. The only liquid that would ever violate its integrity would be spilt wine and even that would not stain the wood.

The boy had become bored with watching wax dry and had disappeared, leaving Stephan to his contemplations. A distant rustling approached him along the terrace and Stephan poked his head out the door frame to see a carpet walking towards him. This was no flying rug from some Oriental opera, for he could see Heinz' shoe buckles sparkling under the burden. Heinz threw off his heavy cape and draped it over the terrace's balustrade. Stephan laughed aloud when Heinz turned to him wielding a long kitchen knife. "Oh kind Sir," Stephan howled in mock terror, "leave me in peace." Heinz raised his left arm to balance the right and thrust the knife towards Stephan in a parody of gentlemen fencing for their honor. They chortled viciously at Heinz' mimicry until Stephan demanded, "Enough of your foolery, boy. What are you up to now?" It was not surprising that Heinz would appear with an old carpet, for Stephan had become used to the boy's magpie scavenging.

Heinz lifted the end of the carpet and cut off a long tail. Stephan was intrigued by what may follow when Heinz cut the remnant in half. He walked to the open door and gently placed the two pieces on the music room floor. "Watch," he commanded to Stephan, and placed both of his feet on the carpet lengths. He pushed himself off and wiggled his body forward.

Stephan watched the boy's shuffling back and his eyes descended to the two gleaming trails Heinz' feet left behind him. The boy's carpeted stride vanquished the dull haze of the wax, leaving a sparkling path. Heinz wove himself forward and the radiance followed him. Heinz twisted his head over his rigid body to examine his progress. Satisfied that his plan was working he pushed himself to the farthest recess of the room and stood balanced with his palms pressed to the wall. He slowly turned to see Stephan gawking from the terrace door along the glimmering path he had ploughed. Heinz returned to his mentor on swaying steps and shouted, "Look, I'm the Baron." Stephan bellowed at Heinz' mimicry of Belfort's mincing prance. "Just like him," Stephan howled through his laughter. Heinz stood beside Stephan savoring the shimmering ribbon.

"Where did you learn to do that?" Stephan asked with genuine admiration. "I didn't," Heinz confessed, "I made it up." Stephan's jaw dropped to think how his apprentice's experiment could have ruined their work and slapped the boy on the shoulder in his relief that it had worked so well. "Now, the student must teach the master," Stephan admitted and stepped across the terrace to the ripped carpet. Heinz' knife soon created two more lengths and brought them to the door. Stephan gingerly placed his feet on the pieces and followed Heinz' lead.

They progressed in a stately tandem to the opposite wall and turned to examine the floor. The swath of light had grown to a wide avenue, inviting them to continue. Stephan attacked the wax with determined strides, and Heinz followed him to wipe at any spots he had missed. They followed the walls to complete the rectangle of the room and only stopped to catch their breaths.

"We must now polish across the grain," Stephan pronounced. "We should dance through our work." When Heinz protested that he knew no dances, Stephan offered to teach him one and gently grasped the youth's hand. Heinz winced at the man's touch. His fear evaporated under Stephan's callused palm. He followed Stephan's first three steps and stood rigid before Stephan's admonishment, "No. No. You are not marching in Retzleff's band of imbeciles. Your feet must glide. Raise your heels and let the front of your feet guide you." Heinz followed and his confidence grew, he could feel the carpet buff the floor beneath him. Stephan sensed the boy's apprehension and said, "Just like when we were caulking the floorboards, take three steps forward." Stephan counted the rhythm "One, two, three," and the motion seemed to seep into Heinz' body and push out his fear of looking stupid. He followed the count with straight-backed obedience. "Now, bend your knees to make a little bow," Stephan whispered. Heinz was starting to enjoy this new game but was very relieved to know that his instruction would not be seen by anybody other than his instructor.

Stephan gently held Heinz' fingers and led off into another three steps. When Heinz acquired command of the first steps, Stephan stopped them and said, "Now, slide your left foot in front of your right and bring it back." He grasped Heinz' hand to steady the boy and watched Heinz' foot glide in a wide semi-circle. "Now, three more steps," and Heinz dutifully obeyed. "This time put your right foot around your left foot and stand." Stephan was pleased with the boy's accomplishment of the rudiments and knew that it would not be very long before the awkwardness of his balance was replaced with a quiet grace.

Stephan led Heinz across the room counting the steps in threes and reminding him which foot to shuffle before the other. He paused their dance to look back and they squinted at the scintillating luster before them. Their steps had burnished the floor into a brilliance that both surprised and delighted Stephan. Before them was a sea of calm brilliance that would put any mirror to shame. He looked down to see his own face smiling back at him and turned to Heinz. "This is a wonderful invention. You have made our work a joy." Heinz puffed with pride and grasped Stephan's hand in thanks. Stephan raised his hand to clasp Heinz' fingertips and took them on a last turn through the music room to end at the terrace door.

He saw the setting sun shroud the hills around the palace and bowed to his apprentice. "Now, it is time for the magic." They stood with the last of the day draining behind them. Stephan commanded Heinz to "Look," and they waited with patient anticipation. The evening sunlight bounded over their shoulders and flooded the room. Before their eyes, the floor raised itself into three dimensional steps. The light pulled the dark squares and light triangles into serried ranks of standing blocks. The whole room looked as though it was filled with geometrical forms hovering before their gaze. Anybody walking into the room would think that he had to mount the stairs that were not really there and be tripped by the illusion. "Only in certain lights will we have this effect. In the middle of the day, it will be just a floor and the pattern will remain flat. At sunset, the whole composition will rise and what was flat and horizontal will become vertical and bold," Stephan explained. Heinz glared in openmouthed wonder at their creation. He knew it was an illusion, but it was more real than anything he had expected. All the time he was working on the floor, he never realized what was growing beneath his very feet. Only, when Stephan allowed the light to play upon the design, did Heinz appreciate the wonder of his master's hidden arts. He adored the old man for this. The very offer of sharing his craft with an unknown boy brought moisture welling into Heinz' eyes. He blinked hard, fearful not only that his tears would be seen, but also that the drops would blemish their achievement.

They stood together in their delight as the sunset crept from the music room, soft as a lullaby sung to a cradle.

Chapter 16

Composition

Quantz sat at his desk, his fingers trembling with rage. He pressed a ruler onto a sheet of paper and grasped a pencil. He had already broken four pencils and each disaster only fueled his anger. He had thrown the last pencil at the wall and retrieved it when he admitted how expensive these maddening sticks could be. He threw down the ruler and attacked the pencil with a knife, not just to restore the point to usefulness, but also to imagine that he was cutting a throat.

It was bad enough that he had to suffer Frederick's insults, but having to contend with Anna's moods was intolerable. The palace may be a snake-infested maze, but he had learned to cope with the courtiers' endless machinations and sordid intrigues. The ostentatious expense of their finery was always a sign of their malice, for the most foppish were the most venomous. He could deafen himself to the smiling calumnies lurking in the whispering galleries. He could ignore the supercilious grins and laugh when they recounted their squalid conquests. But his house was no refuge from the palace when Anna was in the throes of one of her fits. He had to admit that she could start a fight in an empty room. His desk was his only sanctuary and writing music would offer composure. But this night, even the promise of blank staves offered no respite from her torrent of ridiculous abuse.

When the pencil's point was sharp enough to puncture an eye, he set it on the ruler's edge and scribed one bold line across the paper. He moved the ruler down and gouged another line. When he had finished five perfectly straight and properly spaced lines, he cast aside the ruler and pencil to stretch his fingers. The single stave was a start and he listened to his heart, curious to see if calm had returned. His heaving chest told him that there would be many more staves to draw before he could breathe without wishing to do violence. He concentrated on filling the virgin sheet with more staves from top to bottom but he could hear his wife grumbling in the new room below him. When some of the tension seeped out of his body onto the paper, he threw down the pencil, and its point broke again, as if to mock his torment. "Damn them all," he whispered to the wall and slumped into brooding resentment.

Anna stood gasping in her new room, her hands splayed over the top of her new cabinet. She leaned forward to support herself and a drop of sweat fell over her fingers and sank beneath her palm. The wood was so smooth when she wiped the moist drop. She rubbed her fingers together and cursed herself. It was a wonderful piece of furniture, all that she had desired, but she had ruined the gift when Stephan and Heinz delivered her dream.

They had carried the sections from the wagon on the street, through the house, to the new room. First came the legs, sturdily set in their own stout frame. They then delicately man-handled the body of the cabinet to rest upon the legs. Stephan had swung open the doors to reveal the shelves that would hold all of her table cloths and cooking dishes. Stephan had beamed with pride when he told her that they had measured all of her pots and pans and designed each part of the cupboard to hold her treasures. Heinz had proclaimed that he had personally cut each of the grooves with the sharpest chisel. He had demonstrated how his carved runnels would collect any spilt sauce, so she would not have to clean the floor when she was cooking. They had considered her at every stage of the construction and were so happy to explain that this is now truly a cabinet fit for the queen of the house. Quantz stood beaming behind them, wrapped in the pride of being a good provider. When their joy was greeted with her silence, they were confused. Then she simply said, "It's the wrong color." Quantz lost his temper at her ingratitude, and Stephan and Heinz slunk out of the house, shrugging under their disappointment. They escaped through the front door and practically jumped the street to the canal, where they could no longer hear the marital warfare exploding in the house.

Anna's skin tormented her with flaming itches. She looked up to see her face in the mirror Stephan had hung over the cabinet table. The eyes looking back at her were globes of moist reproach. She did not know why she had been so ungracious to Stephan and Heinz, but the accusations she had hurled at her husband flew at her from her reflection. She saw the face of an old woman, terrified by her own mortality. The eyes narrowed in suspicious remorse and she was ashamed of words she had launched at the husband who had worked so hard to give her such finery. When he accused her of ingratitude, she poured scorn over his complaint and reviled him as "no better than one of the King's puppies." She stood staring at his twisted frown, stolid in her triumph, until he simply turned away from her and mounted the stirs.

Her victory was short, to be followed by retreat into her pain. She had walked back into the new room, her heels echoing in her empty kingdom. The cabinet stood throughout the whole ghastly scene, indifferent and waiting. She busied herself by collecting a pair of pots and placed them on the shelves. They sat perfectly fitting the places Stephan had assigned them. The pots rekindled her fury, so she grabbed them by the handles, clanged them together like insane cymbals and threw them across the room.

She trembled as she bent to pick them up. The fatigue simmered through her body, and she grabbed the door handle for support. The handle silently lowered in her hand and the door swung open. It was so perfectly constructed that she didn't have to push for it to swing back along the outside wall. The pots clattered at the door frame and she slumped onto the steps leading to the garden. The night air wrapped her in a calming chill and the zephyrs of night played with the loose strands of her damp hair. She waited for her heart to cease its gallop.

Each breath was an accusation and a question, "Why did I do that?" She looked up at the silent and indifferent moon, but no answer came. There was no telling what she would say. For the past few months, she had grown irritable at the simplest things. She had even cursed a spoon that would not shine under her polishing cloth. She had laughed to herself, but also felt stupid that she was scolding a piece of steel trying to look like silver. She had seen spots appear on her hands and fingers. She looked at the blemishes as if her hands were rotting potatoes, and knew no amount of rubbing would bring back the luster of youth.

Quantz gazed at the page full of staves and thrust it aside with a dismissive wave of his fingers. His fury had abated to a dull resentment but he kept asking himself, "Why did she do that?" He had so hoped the new cabinet would please her. She had started hinting her desire months ago, and he had fumbled coins into his money box to give her the thing she so wanted. There was only enough for half of what it would cost, but then Stephan came to his rescue. "I can do it for much less than the cheats in the stores," he had boasted. Quantz had asked for particulars of this pecuniary miracle, and Stephan had simply exclaimed, "Theft." He had explained in tedious detail how carpentry always produced an excess. He would make sure that the floor he was creating for the music room would harvest enough remnants of planks, shavings, and cuttings to be resurrected as a dresser, "Fit for a queen, since I already stole the wood from the king." Stephan had been true to his word and created a masterpiece out of purloined and discarded refuse. Quantz admired the skill and care Stephan and Heinz had devoted to a piece of furniture and this made his wife's criticism all the more spiteful, cutting, vicious, hurtful, and unkind. He caught himself using different words for the same thought, as if he were mindlessly repeating the same notes.

She had never been easy to live with but, lately, she had been bubbling over with both sweetness and peevish sulkiness. She could change before his eyes and he had not the slightest idea what was happening to her. His mother had died when he was too young to notice the ways of women, and men never spoke of such things. But his shock at her tempers did not impede his quick side-step when she had thrown a pot at him. She would make him a delicious dinner of his favorites and serve it with the utmost solicitude, and then the next night throw down a plate of half-cooked slops with the silent injunction to eat or starve. Besides, to whom could he confide that, "My wife is behaving like a harridan." The men would laugh at him for even noticing and would probably retreat into their belief that the ways of women are not our ways and they are best left to themselves.

He wondered if the appearance of Heinz had something to do with her moods but then remembered that, if anything, Heinz had brought her a welcome serenity. Could it be that the house was too full of people? That she felt more like a women who rented rooms than as a lady of her own domain. The new room disproved his theory, for there was the certain hope that their quarters would expand with the pleasure he provided for the King's amusement. Whatever was happening had her swinging like a pendulum careering between captious accusation and capricious amity. He heard the pots banging below and was glad he had retreated to higher ground.

Anna sat wallowing in her regrets, her body sweltering under the chilly moon. She unhooked the collar strangling her throat and tore apart the buttons and ribbons of the dress that smothered her. Her chest began to settle into a steady rhythm, but she knew there would be a grueling wait for peace. Her swollen feet ached and she pulled off her shoes to stop their torments. She gazed at the plumpness and thought to herself, "If this continues, I shall be walking on turnips." The thought made her giggle, always the first sign that she was returning to the safety of balance. It was the sheer violence of these fits that frightened her most. She could not fathom the cause and thought that her diet was the villain of the piece. No, she admitted. She ate as she always did, so she must find an explanation somewhere other than her stomach. There was also the money, but Quantz was very careful to keep a reserve. She didn't have to beg for coins as did other wives. He was always generous within their limits and grudged her nothing. The shame of her rejection of his generosity filled her with the guilt that clawed at her throat. Some answer would come, but not now. She sat leaning against the doorframe and waited for her feet to stop tormenting her.

Quantz' desk held no such relief. The new flute sat impatient to be played, but Quantz knew that it would have to rest and season itself before it could sing. The Berliner Review was another matter. He scowled at the newspaper's curling pages and the gall rose in his throat. Even the banner made him want to burn the infernal sheets. As if picking at a wound that refused to heal, he read again Kirnberger's slanders on his music. That talentless toady had held Quantz

185

up to ridicule for any idiot foolish enough to believe his nonsense. The personal attack was infuriating in itself, but the assault on Quantz' music demanded a suitable reply. Quantz was condemned for nonconformity to the accepted style. To so blatantly disregard the prevailing craze was tantamount to treason against taste. "A Quantz composition was as passé as it was boring." This was the worst insult Kirnberger could hurl because he was too stupid to appreciate that beauty never fades. Quantz was sure that future generations would see the delicate loveliness of his music when Kirnberger was exposed as the brute who could only mimic storms at sea or write music for fleshly assignations. He chortled to himself when he remembered Stephan's hope that they could adapt Vaucanson's duck to quack in French and fart in German. All they had to do was collect a few violins to play Kirnberger's music while the metal creature clanked through its dance. Then one would be as foul as the other was fowl. He really wanted to shove Kirnberger's head where the mechanical duck performed its finalé. That would be a pretty dance and a fitting end.

Quantz had winced when Kirnberger played his violin at the evening concert. Kirnberger had seen the pained scowl spread over Quantz' face and had asked, "Does the music not please His Majesty's flute maker?" Quantz had replied to the insult by calmly explaining that, "His Majesty is a great lover of music and has the superior sensibility to distinguish between the beauties of an accomplished violinist and a cat being strangled." If it had not been so expensive, Kirnberger would have broken his violin over Quantz' head.

Kirnberger had taken his revenge in a review and offered his private venom to public merriment. Quantz was so incensed that he took the rare step of approaching Frederick. He had demanded that Frederick dismiss Kirnberger from his service and immediately regretted his presumptuousness.

Frederick had savored Quantz' hurt and played on it. Nothing was more dangerous than to allow Frederick to see vulnerability. Frederick heard the request and the wolf's sneer emerged. "God forbid," Frederick said with mock horror. "We must be more intelligent that that. Monsieur Quantz must write something against Monsieur Kirnberger. Thus we will keep an excellent man among us and have an interesting war of words."

So, Quantz was to joust in the lists of the Berliner Review with a dwarf, and all for Frederick's delectation. He could write his own review of Kirnberger's collection of Polish Dances, but he remembered his time in Poland as a court musician and did not wish to besmirch his Polish friends with mock praise of the idiot who had stolen their dances. Quantz wondered if the journal would print an appreciation of Kirnberger's keyboard technique performed by a deaf bear, but rejected the idea as too subtle for the editors.

The insult to Quantz was just another source of entertainment and such contempt for his music was nothing more than a gentleman's duel. Although it was an entertaining fantasy, Quantz could not have Kirnberger quietly strangled, for that would just leave one chair of the orchestra empty to be filled by another dolt. This was Berlin, with some pretensions to civility, not Venice, where a musician could be dumped into the canal.

No. The key was Kirnberger's judgement that, "One does not have to see the name of Herr Quantz to know that the piece is of his composition. The music itself is proof, for it is nothing more than a series of sugar loaves when played and is sure to induce a most desired somnolence."

He threw down the journal. There would be a temporary satisfaction to beating what little sense he possessed in his unworthy head, but Kirnberger would soon be replaced by yet another fawning lackey, equally vapid and possibly

187

worse. No. There had to be another way and that way was readily at hand. Quantz pulled the newly scribed sheets towards him and peered into the gaping staves. "Let the music speak louder than the whip," and picked up the pencil. It felt snug between his thumb and fingers and he held it like a rapier. "So, they don't like my 'sugar loaves,'" he whispered to the sheets and stabbed the first stave three times. He drew his head back to savor the little triplet looking up to him, small and innocent as a kitten. He raised the pencil to attack the next line and repeated the three notes. They were perfect little arcs, rounded at the top like old hills, and Quantz smirked to add more triplets to the line. When he got to the first margin, the kitten had started to purr with satisfaction. He could hear the rhythms careering through his skull and threatening to bring on a headache.

The next line was an inversion of the triplets, as if the first line had collapsed into the crests and troughs of an unquiet sea. The beat became more intense, drumming like early thunder. He could hear Kirnberger's dull thuds of a Bourée and laughed aloud at the childish thumping. "A perfect concerto for an octopus," he growled, and added more triplets and trills to the line.

Let Kirnberger offer His Majesty his simplistic doggerel. He recalled an evening concert just a few weeks ago. Emanuel Bach had been drenching the harpsichord's keyboard with sweat and Benda was practically burping his bow off the strings just to drag some music out of Kirnberger's variations. It was all so dramatic. They could not entertain without twisting their bodies around the notes like soggy pretzels. The royal enthusiasm would soon grow bored with that buffoon's parade of frills.

Quantz' pencil scribed a line of music from one of Kirnberger's flute sonatas, three dull phrases of four quavers.

It was with all the satisfaction of malice that he forced Kirnberger's phrase to an abrupt halt with an arching triplet.

He sat back relishing his musical combat and sensed there was something missing. It was not enough to stab the opponent. Flesh wounds were only marks of honor to the likes of Kirnberger. No. There must be the fatal thrust, clean and lethal. He read through the notes and saw the target. The beginning was soft and set the rest of the piece in a quiet frame. The middle part started to rise beyond Frederick's ability. The end gave Frederick his head, for he loved to play fast, but the notes were beyond both his ability and the limits of his flute. Frederick would have to play this piece on his newest flute if he were not to appear foolish. Quantz added more triplets, black as his mood, making the music gallop like a three-legged horse without a bridle. The rest of the sheet was filled with more triplets vanquishing all before them and rising in a crescendo to a last rest in a finalé of triumphant serenity. When he had finished, he gloated over the deceptive simplicity of his composition. It was so plain, so pure in its clarity as to be a fitting trap for Frederick and Kirnberger. Let them both stumble over the snares he had laid for them.

Anna felt the relief of calm approaching. The storm had passed but the threat of its sudden return held her in its thrall. This was what really frightened her, that she had no control over these fits and less warning. It always started with a tingling in the back of her throat and quickly spread over her face like a virulent rash. The heat could rekindle the glow that would cascade down her neck and fill her chest with unknown fury. Just breathing became a desperate fight for more air than her chest would hold. The dizziness had her grasping at walls to steady herself. It always commenced with a simple cough and soon she would feel that she had crawled into an oven.

She gazed at the moon and begged the full orb for cooling kisses, and as if in answer, a gentle breeze flew over her shoulder. The relief poured through her and left the familiar shame in its wake. She felt the guilt of her tirade against the husband who's only fault was that he was tardy in supplying all her wants. To talk of a color, when he had made such an effort was cheap. The recriminations threatened to fan the embers which so tormented her and she knew there would be relief in apology. But how to do that without making it all worse? She would never throw herself at his feet to beg forgiveness, for that would demand an acknowledgement she could not and would not make. He knew she was stubborn. He understood her moods. Better to let things simmer rather than ignite another altercation.

Quantz picked up the sheet of paper filled with intricate pitfalls and gloated over the tempo. What started as a simple run of notes, mischievously tumbled beyond the novice's abilities and demandied a greater virtuosity. The music was the master. It had always been this way and these notes were another proof that he was their master. Let the likes of Kirnberger sneer at his music. Beauty was always in vogue, for those who could hear the loveliness of the sound. His enemies would have a few more surprises from his hand and would be compelled by the very notes before their ugly faces to admit their inability to play such wonders. The music was as deceptive as their ridicule was ignorant. The music would put them in their places and the little dots and dashes would answer their smirks with a calm and superior challenge. They could read this music, but they could not play it. If Frederick wanted an interesting combat, let him first master the instrument in his own hands.

The pads of his fingers ran over the paper, but he could not remember buying such an expensive folio. His thumb and forefinger gently rubbed the sheet as if it were a suspect coin. The memory of Heinz skipping down the stairs with his serpent burst in his mind. "What was the boy supposed to be doing?" He thought and the memory of Heinz tripping down the palace steps and blasting his hunting call made him realize that the music before him was so much like the rhythm of those youthful feet. He picked up his pencil and added increasing tempos to the little piece he had just composed. "Yes," he thought, "let them trip over the notes where little Heinz, sure-footed as a young goat, could descend with sprightly joy."

"That revolting Belfort," Quantz remembered, "he sent Heinz to retrieve some paper for another of his rambling dissertations." Now, it was clear. Heinz had purloined some of the paper and left it on Quantz' desk. The paper was the boy's way of offering his thanks for kindnesses received, the kindnesses given by Anna. It was so fitting that a charlatan like Belfort should be robbed by a thief who would have the delicacy to leave a gift.

Quantz lay aside the music bearing the new tempo marks, and picked up the flute. He was proud of this latest masterpiece and allowed his fingers to caress the black tube. It was moist to his touch because he had just oiled it. He had drawn a long tail feather of a pheasant through the bore of each section and the instrument glistened. "Patience, My Dear," he assured the tube, "you must bathe for a while before you can sing with mellow wonder."

He heard a soft step on the stairs and winced. She would come up quietly and they would have to meet in reconciliation. Her steps approached and he knew she was standing by the door. Without turning, he roused kindliness to his voice and asked, "Are you feeling any better?" It was the sign that she should not expect the reproach from him that she felt within her.

She walked to the desk to stand beside him, and he felt some of the tension evaporate. This was not the time for accusations. This was not the place to burden themselves with the resentments so freely given and so violently accepted. She picked up the sheet from his desk, and as she read the notes, her brows contracted into a quizzical arch. Quantz looked at her face and smiled to see the skin draw into another sugar loaf. She glanced at the curling corners of his mouth and lingered in the twinkle in his eyes. "This will be a pretty dish to set before the King," she said, hinting at shared mischief.

"He will not be able to play that without this," and he offered her the flute. Her little finger played with the second key he had added to the footjoint. When she released it, the lever made a lively snap that surrounded them. "It will take some time for his fingers to become acquainted with the mechanism," he assured her. "The better for him to master the technique."

He took the sheet of notes from her gentle grasp, placed it on the table and said, "I will make copies for all his palaces. A little reminder that he shall have music wherever he goes." She giggled as he picked up the pencil. With her hand resting on his shoulder, Quantz wrote, "Pour Potsdam" at the head of the notes and relaxed under Anna's touch.

They remained for some time wrapped in silent acceptance of one another, firm in the hope they would not be held captive by their anger.

Chapter 17

Devil in the Box

Heinz stood waiting at the door to the music room. He saw Quantz and the King talking but their words were only a distant and frustrating babble. He held the wooden box in sweaty palms and was terrified that he would drop it. Quantz had adamantly insisted on his taking the greatest care, so Heinz breathed deeply to control his shaking hands. If this thing wriggled from his grip, their hopes would crash, splintered to the floor.

Quantz was in a rare festive mood and his body was as animated as his speech, whatever he was saying. The King was all pleasantries and the royal face beamed with delighted anticipation. Quantz looked away from the King and his hand beckoned Heinz to enter. He walked at a slow and stately pace, just as Quantz had rehearsed him, and thrust his arms forward, offering the box. At each step Frederick's eyes narrowed to Heinz' steady hands until his face could no longer control his expectations of delight. Quantz' smile guided Heinz forward and at the approving nod, he placed the box securely on the King's desk. He stepped back three paces and stood still, relieved that his commission was completed without disaster.

Frederick hovered around the box demanding, "Is this it?" and Quantz assured him that, "Your Majesty will find something very new and, I am quite sure, to your taste." Quantz turned the box toward Frederick and gently pulled back the clasp holding the lid. The top of the box sprang up just slightly and air escaped in a little sigh. "How did you make that happen?" Frederick asked. Quantz' grin of satisfaction launched his answer, "From your snuff boxes."

"How snuff boxes?"

"You have given away so many of those exquisite boxes that I thought it was time you received one yourself. I took the liberty of examining one and saw that there was a very cunning relationship between the hinges and the clasp which held the lid in place."

Frederick was intrigued by the box's lid. He kept looking at it for some hidden surprise. His fingers pressed the lid until he heard the click of the latch securing it to the body. He poked the front with an enquiring forefinger and the lid jumped open. Quantz watched Frederick repeat the process with increased joy at every opening. The same delight shone from the King's eyes as when a child plays with his own Devil-in-the-Box, squealing with every appearance of the puppet flying from the box. But no devil appeared to scare a credulous infant. The opening revealed the sections of Frederick's latest flute with more promise than fear.

"When one opens one of those snuff boxes, the top springs up to offer its fragrant contents," Quantz explained. "Why not have the same offering for a flute case? What is good for the nose is even better for the ear."

Frederick exploded into giggles and covered his mouth like an embarrassed girl. Quantz inclined his head to Heinz as the signal for the boy to make himself scarce. Heinz bowed low with a sweeping wave of his arm that seemed to amuse the King. He backed his way to the door, thrust one foot behind him, turned like a drunken ballerina, and disappeared through the door. On the terrace, he stood amid the cloud of chortles at his exit, patiently waiting for his next command. Quantz and the King ignored him listening to their every word. When servants became invisible, the masters were both seen and heard.

Frederick bent over his table and his eyes darted over each section of the flute. The box was shallower than his other flute cases for it contained compartments for only four sections. Frederick's face squashed into a question, "Where are the other sections?"

"The other parts are now not necessary, for there is no need to change the composition of the instrument for different pitches," Quantz assured Frederick.

"But will I not need more parts to play in tune with the orchestra?" Frederick queried.

"I have thought long about this matter of tuning the instrument and have decided that there is no need for the instrument to be in tune with other instruments."

"Will that not make a terrible sound?" Frederick objected.

"The other sections are only required when the player is to act in concert with the other musicians. In this case, the other instruments must tune themselves to the flute."

Frederick looked puzzled, until he realized that Quantz' magnificent craft had not only given him a marvelous instrument but also made the other players subservient to that instrument.

Quantz sensed the change in Frederick's mood and showered his royal pupil with most pleasing instruction. "Separate sections for tuning are necessary for a traveling musician going from town to town and never knowing the pitch to be employed. Your Majesty is no itinerant journeyman of music. As the instrument is subject to you, so is the orchestra subject to the instrument. They will tune to your pitch."

Frederick nodded his enthusiastic agreement, for this flute raised him from King in Prussia to the monarch of the orchestra. Quantz' new instrument was altogether fitting to Frederick's talent but also to his station. He was impatient to fill the tube with his breath.

"Examine the parts. You will discover new surprises."

Frederick removed each of the sections from the case and reverently placed them on his desk. One of the central tubes started to roll to the edge of the desk until Quantz caught it between expert fingers. Frederick looked up sheepishly at Quantz' impassive face and quickly arranged the pieces so they would not crash to the floor. Frederick picked up the footjoint and exclaimed, "What is this?"

"This," Quantz revealed, "is a new invention."

His finger pointed to an extra lever he had attached over another hole he had bored through the wood."

"But what does it do?" Frederick whined in impatience.

"When you play, all will be revealed."

That was the signal for Quantz' permission for Frederick to assemble his new flute. As was his habit, Frederick married the two middle sections together and lined up the six holes to match his fingers. Quantz coughed when Frederick jammed the headjoint onto the middle sections as if he were fixing a bayonet to a musket. Frederick, obedient to Quantz' throaty complaint, removed the headjoint and replaced it with greater care.

He picked up the footjoint and examined the extra key which Quantz had added. He pressed the lever and the little key jumped up and down over the hole. Frederick was at a loss to know just what this new addition did.

"How should I assemble this new flute?"

"Exactly as you always do."

Frederick carefully placed the footjoint onto the bottom tenon of the body and waited for Quantz' approval. Quantz nodded and commanded, "Now sound one note."

Frederick obeyed and a clear and luscious sound filled the room. They stood for a moment, bathed in the reverberations of the solitary note. Frederick reveled in the sound he had made. This instrument was superior to anything he had ever held and that single note was a herald promising yet more hidden joys. His fingers tingled with possibilities and his hands shook with the eagerness to continue Quantz' latest invitation to the adventures he so loved. He must surrender to his master if all the mysteries of this new flute were to be revealed to him. He fingered the footjoint and with controlled and feigned nonchalance asked, "And what does this do?"

Quantz' lips compressed into the satisfaction an angler feels when there is the slightest tug on his line. The lever of the new key gleamed in alluring and silent invitation. "Play a scale and see," Quantz suggested.

Frederick thrust out his arms to pull his sleeves free of his hands and raised the flute to his face. He blew twice to warm the headjoint and they were surrounded by a spluttering flutter of air. He raised questioning brows to Quantz, who responded with an encouraging and permissive nod. Frederick raised each finger of his right hand and Quantz was slightly annoyed that he was pumping his elbow at each note, as if the angle of his arm would help sustain the clarity of each note. Quantz would wait to discipline this lazy habit before it became an impediment to Frederick's playing, but now was not the time to intrude upon his student's enjoyment. When the sound was progressing up the scale through the three open holes, Frederick lurched slightly forward and started to lift the fingers of his left hand. Quantz knew what would happen next but his face betrayed not the slightest hint of foreknowledge. He waited with gleeful patience for Frederick's fingers to fall into the usual trap. Frederick continued to ascend the scale until he reached the point where he had to depress the key on the footjoint and open the hole.

They could hear the awkwardness of the note fill the room. Frederick's fingers flew between two notes and the little key quivered on every second sounding. "It sounds terrible," he complained with a hint of shame that he was responsible for this annoying sound.

"And so it should," Quantz proclaimed.

"I was under the impression that each note should be a thing of beauty in itself," Frederick grumbled.

"And that beauty is in the second key," Quantz assured him. "Now play the same note, but this time, use only the lever on the second key."

Frederick obeyed and the note rang clear and full. He stood back examining the new arrangement of keys on the footjoint.

"Now, play the same note using only the old key," he advised.

Frederick complied with added attention and the note that was so dissonant crept mockingly out of the flute. "Yes," Quantz sighed, "is it not a thing of ugliness? So out of place with the notes on either side of it."

"Should not such a sound be banished?" Frederick asked.

"Even that which is ugly has its purposes. No. Save it for a time when you wish for it to be in the service of beauty. These notes are at your command. Why discard something which you may one day wish to use?"

Frederick accepted the wisdom of retaining something which would be to his advantage. Unlike intriguing courtesans, he could hardly deport one note to France. His attention soon returned to this new configuration of keys. They would have to be mastered and he was eager for more instruction.

"The same note, only with the new key," Quantz commanded.

Frederick immediately heard the difference between the two notes. The new key removed the burr from the sound. With this key, he could produce a purer, more pleasing, and smoother sound. Quantz' innovation was very much like a sharpened plane removing the excess grain from a piece of wood. When he played the scale with the new key, the line was as neat and accurate as the finest lace.

Quantz saw Frederick's fingers fidget with the new key. Frederick raised and lowered his little finger, as if stabbing the key. Quantz knew this would be rectified with practice, but he had to ensure that Frederick knew what he was doing, so he could practice with increased dexterity and not just repeat the mistakes he was trying to cure.

"Move the finger horizontally," he suggested.

Frederick followed and his finger protested this new manner of playing. Quantz made him slide his finger between the keys. He told Frederick that the hand movement would be easier if he moved his fingers from the wrist and dispensed with the exaggerated motions of the right elbow. When Frederick relaxed his arm and felt more at ease, his hand did all of the work. He made Frederick play the scale one last time and they listened to its echo in the room. Quantz complimented. "That is much better." Frederick was awed by the undeniable improvement in clarity. He wished he could capture this sound and Quantz told him that this improvement in his technique would ensure that he could repeat the sound at will. There was no need to cage it. "Why is it so much better?" Frederick inquired with the humility that Quantz had come to recognize in his student. "Now you are playing the flute and not pumping a bagpipe." Frederick cast aside the restraints of ceremony and laughed uproariously at the image of him beating a tune out of a pig's bladder. Quantz shared in the merriment until he decided that Frederick was ready for more.

"Let us experiment with some real music," Quantz said, and placed one of Frederick's sonatas on the music stand. Frederick jumped as if meeting an old friend and started one of his own compositions that they had played many times before. Quantz let Frederick enjoy his performance and watched carefully how the flute responded to new fingers. He saw Frederick's breath splutter until the mouthole misted over. This was a sure sign that Frederick was wasting air.

He allowed Frederick to finish and while Frederick was basking in his achievements, Quantz took the flute from his grasp. "Now we must settle that annoying little problem," he said.

"And which one his that?"

"The breath," Quantz stated. "Put your hand close to your mouth vertically with the fingers spread." Frederick obeyed and his stance looked like he was suggesting that they hush. His eyes delved into Quantz' gaze to discover what wonders were in store for him.

"Now, blow onto your hand as if you are blowing into the flute," Quantz said.

Frederick was enjoying this new game and waited for instruction.

"Thrust your chin out and then in and tell me what you feel in your hand."

Frederick's breath spluttered over his palm and warbled through his fingers. "When I push the chin out, the air flies over my hand. When I pull in the chin, the air blows under the hand."

"Excellent," Quantz assured him, "Now, blow between each of your fingers, very slowly, but only use your chin to direct the air."

Frederick worked his face and his hands until he could direct the flow of the air over and under his hand and through his fingers. Quantz returned the flute and told him to, "Play the same scale, but think that you are blowing through your fingers to get more breath into the instrument."

Frederick played the scale with ease and confidence. By simply controlling the flow of air he was able to change the accuracy of the tone. Quantz was satisfied that Frederick would be able to manipulate both the new key and the improved embouchure. Long experience had taught Quantz that three new skills were enough for a satisfying lesson. Frederick had received two new elements and awaited the third.

"We must now tune the whole instrument," Quantz proclaimed and his eyes suggested yet more gifts. "Please disassemble the instrument and put it on your desk."

Frederick delicately separated the four parts of his flute and the pieces waited patiently before them. Quantz reached into the flute case and retrieved four wooden rings. He put them on the table and Frederick was intrigued by the little metal circles. "What will these do?" he asked.

Quantz grinned and instructed, "Place two of these rings over the tenon in the middle of the flute." Frederick obeyed and Quantz told him to reassemble the flute. When the instrument was complete he asked Frederick for another scale. Instantly, Frederick heard that the pitch of the whole instrument had subtly changed.

"There is no need to rebuild the flute for every pitch. With these little rings, you are now able to able to raise and lower the whole pitch by simply adding or subtracting the rings."

Frederick realized that Quantz had devised a solution to a problem that was as elegant as it was simple. He admired the man's nimble mind that could design answers to the questions that evaded others. He stood to play again and Quantz felt satisfied with his handiwork.

"There is a secret lurking in the headjoint," Quantz suggested. Frederick looked at the end of the flute but could see no difference.

"Sound a note and twist the little knob you will feel with your hand."

Frederick blew another note and his fingers discovered a tiny ferule. He turned this unobtrusive knob with his thumb and forefinger and the sound changed slightly.

"By manipulating the rings and the screw you will be able to tune the whole instrument as you desire."

"Would not the pitch depend on some objective scale?" Frederick asked.

"In Prussia, you are the scale. Therefore, the flute will be tuned to your ear."

Frederick puffed with the knowledge that he was the absolute ruler of the music. Quantz grinned and confided, "You courtiers scramble for the king's ear. Now the king's ear controls the courtiers."

Frederick's laughter threatened to flood the flute, so Quantz took it from his hands and waited for the spasms of giggling to subside.

Quantz wondered if Frederick could accept any more of his surprises, so he held the flute in one hand and searched the flutecase with the other. Frederick watched Quantz carefully lay the flute on the desk, take a small bottle out of his pocket and open it. "This is almond oil," Quantz said. He took a long feather from the flutecase and shook a few drops of oil over it. Frederick watched enchanted as Quantz pushed the feather into the flute from the lower end. "This instrument is virgin. We must lubricate it so that the wood remains moist. If the wood becomes dry, the sound will be terrible. But we must allow a few days for the oil to penetrate. Please do not play it until the oil has completed its task. A little patience now will bear much fruit."

They sat silent, for there was nothing else to say. Frederick stared at his new flute as if he expected it to rise and play itself. The wood beckoned him, but he knew he had to obey Quantz' injunction to just leave it alone and allow the oil to work its magic.

Quantz sensed that Frederick wanted more, but he would no go beyond his accustomed three parts of the lesson. Anything more would be an avalanche and Frederick would suffocate under too much instruction. But he also knew that he was needed for more than music.

"We have played so much fine music together," Quantz sighed.

"Yes," Frederick recalled. "It is a great joy."

"One that grows greater with the years."

He knew that Frederick was searching for something from the past and this made him bold to go where only the king's eyes invited him.

"When we first played together, the other monarchs claimed that you were only a king in Prussia."

Frederick's eyes flashed with a hatred so intense that Quantz had to continue.

"That was as much an insult to Prussia as it was to you. Then you added more territory to Prussia and the monarchs were forced to recognize you as the 'King of Prussia'."

Quantz appreciated the satisfaction that Frederick felt in the expansion of his kingdom and the recognition of his kingship. Quantz picked up the flute and held it before Frederick as if it were a marshall's baton fit only for victorious hands.

"This is an instrument," Quantz proclaimed, "fit for an emperor. It would give me the greatest satisfaction if you named it 'The Emperor's Flute'."

Frederick took the flute from Quantz' proffered hands and held it close to him. "This is a title which I am honored to bequeath." He sat with his new honor resting in his hands and Quantz waited for he knew not what. He only perceived that he was needed, so he waited upon the King.

"If only my sister could play with this flute," Frederick almost whined.

203

"It has been quite some time since I have had the exquisite pleasure of our trios with the Princess Wilhelmina."

"Since her marriage, there is no time for music."

"But surely there is music in Bayreuth?" Quantz asked, "Wherever Wilhelmina goes, music is sure to follow her."

"But Bayreuth is such a long way away. We will never be able to play together as we did as children."

"Those were good times," Quantz recalled with sincerity.

Frederick's eyes narrowed as he put the flute on his desk. He rose, paced slowly to a cabinet and returned with a military dispatch box. He turned a little key and pried open the lid with a protesting squeal. No wooden devil popped out of the box, but Frederick withdrew two sheets of music. "I have a little composition for her," and offered the music to Quantz. "Tell me what you think."

Quantz read the two pages of music and immediately appreciated how bad it was. The tune was childish and the simplicity of the melody was something he would expect from an apprentice with little knowledge. To say that it was beneath Frederick's abilities was a gross understatement. He really could not fathom what he was looking at. "As the workmen would say of their previous work, 'It's a lovely piece'."

"Yes," Frederick conceded, "I am sure that Wilhelmina could play it on the harpsichord and improve it, cunningly."

Quantz sensed there was something more lurking as a trap to be avoided, but he didn't know just what it was. Frederick waited until he was sure of Quantz' submission.

"If only I could get it to her," he sighed.

"I am sure that a messenger could deliver it with all haste," Quantz said.

"I do not wish to entrust this to a courier," Frederick said with some heat.

Quantz looked carefully at the notes. Something stirred in his memory so he hummed the tune to himself. When he could hear it in his head, he knew it was one of the songs Frederick had composed with his sister when they were children. That explained the simplicity of the music but not the emergency of its delivery. He looked into the pattern of the notes and remembered that Frederick and Wilhelmina used to put secrets into their music. They would play and laugh until Quantz had to ask the reason for their amusement. Wilhelmina had explained that two sets of triplets meant their father had gas. The music was not only an act of defiance of their tyrant, but was also their only means to express their contempt. It was their little secret.

Now he understood. The music was no mere diversion for a bored queen. There was something of importance in these two sheets which Frederick wished to communicate to his sister, now Queen Wilhelmina of Bavaria. This was not music. This was a code.

"I could deliver the piece to Wilhelmina," Quantz suggested with studied calm.

"That would be wonderful," Frederick assented. "You know she thinks you the God of Music."

Quantz gazed into Frederick's eyes and those moist orbs blurred with memories of times that never were and fear of things he hoped would never be.

"As I know her to be a true friend," Quantz replied.

Quantz grasped the appreciation in Frederick's voice but it was not greater than Quantz' relief. The paper in his hand held the key to many problems and one of them was hiding in his house.

"I will give you an escort," Frederick assured him.

"Would not an escort draw attention to the messenger? It would be more fitting and less suspicious if a simple musician and palace servant traveled alone by the public coach."

Frederick saw the sense in Quantz suggestion. He knew there were many spies in his kingdom and Quantz was the soul of discretion. He could deliver the message without drawing any attention to himself.

"What will you need for the journey?" Frederick asked.

"As I will be traversing the kingdom's borders, all that is required is a pass from your hand. All else is at my disposal."

"When can you go?" Frederick demanded.

"If I start in the morning, I can journey the three days to Bayreuth and Queen Wilhelmina will have a new composition."

"Excellent," Frederick exclaimed, and it was the signal for Quantz to take his leave.

"I have only one request, Your Majesty," he said.

"Anything, Quantz."

"I must take the flute with me to make final adjustments."

"All the way to Bayreuth?" Frederick asked.

"Oh, no," Quantz assured him. "I will oil the instrument at home and return it to you before I leave."

"I can become accustomed to it during your journey," Frederick beamed.

Quantz almost begged Frederick, "Please do not play the flute until my return. It will take that long for it to mellow."

Frederick nodded and Quantz bowed to leave the presence.

He stepped through the door onto the terrace and Heinz scampered to walk by his side. Heinz was confused by Quantz' gruff manner but attended to the commands. "Find Stephan. Take him home. I will arrive shortly. Now run, you little scamp."

Heinz knew when not to dally. Quantz breathed relief as he watched Heinz run down the steps of the palace on his way to Potsdam.

Chapter 18

The Road Not Taken

Stephan puffed behind Heinz through Potsdam's streets. He wheezed to his young and healthy apprentice, "Slow down." Heinz fell into a walk, so Stephan could catch his breath. He knew that two men hurrying home in the afternoon would cause heads to turn. Whatever Quantz was up to was Quantz' business and of no concern to the people sauntering from shop to shop searching for bargains and gossip.

When they approached the house, Heinz casually looked along the street, searching for curious eyes. Usually, he could not care less what people saw, but this evening he was acutely aware that those eyes were placed above mouths containing tongues that would cheerfully wag to the police for any advantage. He could barely contain his own desire to know what was going on, but he relied on the patience which had always defended him from harm. He held the door open for Stephan and gently closed it when Anna appeared to confront them. "Why are you here so early? You won't get fed until I have finished."

Stephan slumped into a chair in the kitchen and Anna sensed that food was not what he needed. She drew a tankard from the masons' barrel and thrust it to him. He grasped it with more than thirst and when she saw Heinz' disappointment, grabbed another tankard for the boy. They were sweating and that could only mean some urgency hidden from her. "What has happened?" she demanded.

"Master told me to bring Stephan here," Heinz said calmly between gulps.

"Just bring him here?" Anna queried with annoyance.

"Yes," Heinz responded with a suggestion that Quantz' command was all that was necessary for him to obey. Stephan was as eager to find out what Quantz was plotting as the others but a long life of service had taught him when to keep his ears open and his mouth discreetly shut.

Anna pressed Heinz, "Is that all he said?" Before Heinz could answer Quantz himself filled the front door and walked down the corridor to the kitchen. When they looked up to him, all he said was, "Good. You're here." He swung his gaze over them and demanded, "Where is Defutois?" Anna rose and squeezed past him with the assurance, "I'll get him."

Quantz pulled up a chair, looked at Stephan's tankard and said, "As our mason friends say, 'This is thirsty work,'" Stephan chortled as Heinz jumped to fill a tankard for Quantz.

Quantz pulled back his wig, broke the thread tying it to his coat, and cast it on the table. He stroked his sweaty scalp with one hand and quaffed a long draught of beer with the other. He felt the liquid soothe his dry throat and ease his jitters. He was as nervous as when he had to play a solo, so he drank and allowed the stream to calm him. When he heard four footsteps descend the stairs, he looked up to see Anna leading Defutois into the kitchen. He calmly placed the tankard on the table and said, "Ah, a relief to see you, Frenchman."

Anna placed a chair behind Defutois and he was glad to accept the invitation to sit and join them. Quantz pushed his tankard over the table and Anna drew a new draught for Defutois. They all sat waiting for what they knew would be important news, but were careful to follow Quantz' lead.

He looked directly at Defutois and pronounced, "Young Man, you are going on a journey." They all sighed relief, but Defutois, desperate for deliverance, begged Quantz for more, "Back to France?" he asked.

"Yes, but by a new route," Quantz explained. "You and Heinz will walk to Berlin tonight. Heinz, tomorrow morning, you will go to a coaching inn across the river. I forget the name."

"I think it is called the Golden Lion," Heinz added.

"Yes, that's it," and Quantz asked suspiciously, "You know this place?"

"A little," Heinz replied and fell frustratingly silent.

That Heinz should know about such an establishment forced even more questions into Quantz' mind, but for now, all that was needed was for Heinz to know the place and lead Defutois to the inn.

Heinz turned all his attention to hear Quantz' orders, "During the day, you will find a coachman who is willing to take us to Bayreuth."

"That's far away," Heinz observed.

"And expensive," Quantz added. "I will make sure you have the money to hire his services and his vehicle."

Stephan was completely surprised by the mention of their destination. "That's a journey of three days," he protested.

"A journey for young legs and a king's messenger. You will stay here."

"Why are we making this journey?" Heinz added.

"I am going to Bayreuth to speak with the king's sister. You will disappear."

"In Bayreuth?" Heinz said.

"I will stay at the palace. You will continue through Bavaria until you arrive at the border of Switzerland."

"The guards will stop us," Heinz said.

"Heinz, My Dear, You will not cross the border, but Defutois will."

"That is impossible without the proper papers," Defutois protested.

Quantz took a folded parchment from his pocket and cast it on the table to Defutois. When it was unfolded, it revealed a request to "Offer all assistance to the bearer of this as to satisfy the king's pleasure," over the signature, "Frederick, King of Prussia."

They sat staring at the piece of paper, knowing it was their own passport. Stephan knew it was useless to ask how he had acquired such a wonder, for Quantz was most effective when his lips were the tightest.

Defutois had taken in Quantz' commands but was unsure that this was the best way. "I have to return to France through Switzerland?" he demanded.

Anna looked piqued by the young man's lack of gratitude and told him bluntly. "Would you rather be buried in Prussia?"

"But that is a very strange route to travel," Defutois protested to Quantz' annoyance. "Why can I not just travel the road west? In a mere two days I will be in France."

"The road west will be blocked," Quantz countered.

"How can that be?"

"The hussars will be looking for you," Anna explained, "especially on that road."

"Because it is the most direct and quickest route."

Because it is the same road Frederick took," Stephan blurted.

Quantz was annoyed and clicked his tongue to Stephan to remain silent.

"I don't understand," Defutois grumbled. "And why is this straight road so difficult?"

"Frederick was arrested on that same road when he was younger than you," Anna told him.

"How can a king be arrested?" Defutois demanded.

"It is the king who does the arresting when it is a prince and his own son who is arrested," Anna added.

Quantz sighed and capitulated to what he knew was a forbidden subject. Everybody knew what had happened on the road to France when Frederick was a young prince. And everybody who valued his life knew never to speak of those events. The tale was buried under purposeful forgetfulness. To remember was almost as dangerous as to talk. Quantz sensed that Defutois had to know the full story. Defutois could prattle the story in France but if he spoke about what they were going to tell him, in Prussia it would be too late for them all. In a few days, Defutois would be safe and they would be rid of the danger he posed. Quantz looked directly at Defutois and informed him, "King Wilhelm was Frederick's father. He was a very cruel tyrant."

"He was cruelest to his own family," Anna recalled.

"King Wilhelm hated everything French, so Frederick dressed in forbidden fashions and played French music," Stephan said.

"The music was the worst," Quantz remembered. "The father claimed the music made Frederick effeminate. Frederick started playing his flute in secret. He had a young girl play harpsichord."

"She was a baker's daughter," Anna added, "and King Wilhelm got it into his head that the girl had plans to marry the prince."

"He had the girl flogged through the streets of Berlin," Stephan said sadly. "The hangman tied her to the back of a wagon and whipped her through the city. Poor girl had no back when they finished with her."

"All for playing a harpsichord?" Defutois exclaimed.

"All for defying the King," Anna warned him. "Frederick could no longer bear his father's humiliations so he decided to run away."

"All children do that," Defutois said.

"Yes, but very few are the children of a Prussian King seeking shelter from the King of France who is also the enemy of the King of Prussia," Quantz said.

"He escaped with his lover, von Katte," Stephan told him.

"We do not speak of such things," Quantz exploded.

"We should," Anna objected. "He should know so he will take care."

"Especially now that the von Katte is out of the bag," Stephan quipped.

Quantz was outraged that Stephan would go further into the story than was necessary, but there was little he could do. "Von Katte," Quantz continued, "was Frederick's best friend. They were inseparable companions. I once had to hide in a closet with von Katte when King Wilhelm stormed into Frederick's rooms and destroyed his books and instruments in a fit."

"The Old King was very dangerous," Anna added. "He horsewhipped Jews in the streets. Terrible."

"This was the father?" Defutois asked in breathless astonishment.

"What happened was worse," Stephan sighed.

"They were caught on the very border of the kingdom. Wilhelm charged them both with treason and was determined to have them executed."

"His own son?"

"And his heir."

"What did he do?" Defutois begged.

"Wilhelm imprisoned them both for months. Eventually he was convinced by the Chancellor to show mercy to his son. No mercy was extended to von Katte."

Defutois knew there would be something more terrible than a whipping. He wanted to cover his ears but Quantz' telling compelled Defutois attention.

"Frederick was kept in the prison," Quantz sadly recalled. "Wilhelm had a scaffold raised to the height of Frederick's window. The guards restrained Frederick in a chair. A soldier, one of the Giants, held open Frederick's eyes so he could watch von Katte being beheaded."

"I made that scaffold," Stephan remembered, with more hate than pity in his voice. "So much blood. I had to burn all the wood."

"Frederick was forced to watch this murder?" Defutois demanded.

"On the orders of his own father," Quantz told him with a shudder.

They sat silent in the horror of those awful words. Quantz was filled with the hurt he had felt many years ago. Anna was glad they had spoken of this awful thing. Now, no one could ignore the truth wrapped in silence. Stephan dropped his head in resignation of their complete impotence in the face of such power. Heinz was silent, hearing only confirmation of what he had always guessed about the barons and their masters.

Defutois looked to Quantz, as if to thank him. The tale spoke of the depth of his own vulnerability. If they would flog a girl for playing music and take the head of a beloved friend, they could do with him as they pleased. There was no law to restrain such vindictiveness. No code of decency softened the cruelty of their vengeance. If he fell into their clutches, Defutois could only look to death to end the pain they would inflict upon him. He sat petrified by the terror of knowing that the will of the King is the law of the land.

Chapter 19

Furioso

Frederick walked along the corridor to the music room, eager for the evening concert. He would play his old flute and leave Quantz' newest masterpiece to mature. He had thoroughly prepared the music and his mood bristled with assurance that this would be a most satisfying performance. He wished his sister could hear him, but she would understand the music and its message as soon as Quantz delivered the notes to her.

He could hear happy noises coming from the music room. There was joy punctuated with hilarity and he could tell that the musicians were entertaining themselves. This was also a good sign, for when the orchestra was refreshed, the music was superior. He opened the door and a barrage of laughter greeted him.

The musicians stood on his entrance and assumed more somber expressions. Benda raised himself to his full, squat height, grasping his violin as if he were strangling a chicken. Graun was tall and looked like he was about to tumble over his low bow. Carl Philipp Emanuel Bach stood casually at his harpsichord with his usual supercilious grin but was having some difficulty controlling his glee. The other musicians always called him 'Emanuel' because this name annoyed him, but he was always just 'Bach' to Frederick, who liked to remind his harpsichordist that he was not as famous nor as accomplished as his more celebrated father. The evening concert was always a joy to the King, because it was a cockpit for the musicians.

Frederick bid them, "Good evening, Gentlemen," and cast a curious eye over his troupe. "I am so happy to see you all in such a gay mood. May I inquire as to the cause of this merriment?" They all shuffled like schoolboys caught in a prank and Frederick's face beamed with the possibilities of a joke. Benda giggled, Graun grinned, but Bach shuffled in uncertainty. "Benda," Frederick invited, "what have you been doing?"

"Not I, Your Majesty," and Benda shook his violin in the general direction of Bach. Frederick narrowed his gaze onto his harpsichordist as if he were taking aim. Bach threw an accusing grimace at the violinists and Graun informed Frederick that, "Bach has just shared a most amusing anecdote." Benda added that, "It is a very funny riddle."

Frederick leered at Bach and demanded, "Please share the riddle with us, Bach. I enjoy having my mind stimulated with this most amusing manner of mental exercise."

Graun and Benda were enjoying Bach's discomfort and Benda was quick to say, "The riddle is 'what is the most powerful animal in the Prussian dominions?'"

Frederick made a great play of stroking his chin and deciphering the conundrum. "I would have to say the cavalry horse, because the noble steed's determination is such as to increase the domains of Prussia. This horse expands the kingdom. Therefore, it must be the most powerful beast in the kingdom."

Graun shook his head and explained. "A most excellent answer which, as the subject matter, expands the kingdom of our knowledge as a good riddle should."

Benda also informed Frederick, "But that is not Bach's answer to the riddle."

"And what is the answer, if my solution is incorrect?" Frederick demanded.

Bach's tongue would not move. He was rooted to the floor as if Stephan had left an excess of glue to catch his feet. Frederick waited, enjoying Bach's distress until Bach was forced to say, "This formidable creature is Madame Quantz' lap-dog."

Frederick stared at Bach in confusion, suspecting that there was another trap beyond his knowledge. "And just how does Madame Quantz enjoy such a reputation?" he inquired.

Bach was silent, so Benda added the next line of the riddle. "Such is its power that Madame Quantz herself is afraid of it."

Frederick's lips pursed into amusement and he looked to Graun for more. Graun's eyes fixed on Bach as he said, "Quantz is afraid of Madame Quantz." Frederick followed Graun's stare to Bach. The moments felt like tortured hours until Frederick broke the silence and challenged Bach. "And what is the right answer?"

Benda and Graun waited with nervous anticipation for Bach to plummet into Frederick's trap. Bach knew he must answer and feared the consequences. Frederick aggressively cocked his ear until Bach mumbled, "And Frederick, the greatest monarch in the world, is afraid of Quantz."

Frederick smiled at the terror playing across Bach's crimson face. Benda and Graun relaxed as if the hounds had captured their quarry and were waiting for the kill. Bach's feet felt the floor as if he would find an escape in its confusing pattern.

Frederick's laughter exploded and he spluttered, "Madame Quantz' lap-dog." They all sighed the relief of the damned to see Frederick laugh so heartily at Bach's anecdote. Frederick approached the music stand and kept giggling and repeating, "Madame Quantz' lap-dog." When he picked up his old flute, the musicians sat and assumed their positions to play their master's composition. Bach's chair squealed when he sat at the harpsichord and his hands quivered above the keys. Frederick blew one note and they all started to play until the flute sprayed royal spittle over them all and

Frederick shouted, "Madame Quantz' lap-dog." He repeated the title a few more times with mounting hilarity and they waited for his fit to subside and the music flow.

Frederick played with greater gusto than usual and Benda wondered if the joke had inspired the speed of Frederick's performance. Within a few bars, Frederick pulled the flute from his lips and shouted to Bach, "This is written con spirito. You are not playing a dirge at Madame Quantz' funeral." Bach waited until Frederick demanded, "Again, from the beginning." They all poised to follow their master's musical lead. Benda sensed the annoyance in Frederick's tone was the mere prelude to an outrage. His chin clutched his violin and his eyes bored into the notes on his music stand as if he were searching for an escape. Graun was stoic in his playing, strangely subdued, trying to hide in the music.

Bach increased the tempo, but this only incensed Frederick. "What is wrong with you?" Frederick shouted to the harpsichord as if he did not want to even look at the player. "Con spirito," he shot at the instrument, "Risoluto." Bach hurried as Frederick insisted but his sweaty fingers slipped over the keys until he was sounding two notes where only one should be. Strange chords of fearful and barely controlled panic rose from his hands. His efforts to comply only infuriated Frederick all the more. "Don't you understand basic Italian?" he accused Bach. "Spirito means 'spirited' not 'stupid', you fool. Even the most ignorant village idiot understands risoluto means 'bold and strong' but even this is beyond you."

Bach sat with his hands above the keys, his fingers tight and pulled apart as if he were a skeleton grasping for a throat. "Again," Frederick commanded and they returned to the start of the piece, but even this would not satisfy Frederick. "You have become fat and lazy. I pay you too much. I will give you exercise. I shall leash you to a horse and run you to

Berlin. Then you will know the tempo I demand," Frederick screamed.

Frederick stomped around the room waving his arms in a frenzy, demanding greater speed with each motion. They tried in desperation to follow his fist rising and falling in ever more violent thumps, as if he were about to strike them. Benda's middle finger started to bleed and Graun's bow arm swung wildly as if he were a maniac woodsman sawing through a tree. A bead of sweat dropped from Bach's nose to soil the keys and trip his fingers.

Frederick paced closer to them, his arm hammering the air before him. As he passed his desk, the cuff of his sleeve caught the end of his new flute. The music stopped abruptly as they all watched the flute rise into the air, somersault in a graceful turn, tumble to the edge of the desk, and crack to the floor in two pieces.

Frederick bent in horror. His wonderful instrument was sliced in half. He watched each piece tremble until it came to rest, silent, a dead thing that had promised him such pleasure.

"What will Quantz say?" Frederick wailed. "I promised him I would not play it." He looked at the musicians, his terror bubbling through tears. "He will think that I broke my word," he whimpered.

Bach's nostrils expanded in fear. Benda sat immobile and Graun felt a strange sorrow at Frederick's plight. Frederick picked up the pieces and held them in supplicating hands. He turned on Bach and was about to attack his harpsichordist with the broken flute. "This is all your fault," he shrieked. "You will pay for this."

Frederick stood before them moaning. "If I assure Quantz I was not playing it, he will not believe me," he moaned, "Oh, What is to be done?"

Frederick staggered back to his desk and gently placed the pieces together. They rested and he gazed upon his hopes as if mourning twin children taken early by a cruel and remorseless fate.

He sat and pulled paper and pen towards him. The musicians watched him scribble and the scratching of his pen was like a knife scraping their bones. He threw the pen into the inkwell and commanded them, "Come here."

They abandoned their instruments and obeyed. "You will all read and sign this," Frederick told them. They could hardly believe the words flying around them. The paper was witness to their "inconsiderate stupidity in that they had disturbed His Majesty's pleasure and in the process had ruined his treasured instrument."

They stood in hardened and astonished perplexity, but all signed their master's statement that they were responsible for breaking the flute. Bach signed last, fearful that the pen would blot the paper and he would have to sign another paper stating that he had ruined the first paper.

Frederick peered at their signatures and his eyes cast nothing but contempt over the band of miscreants. "I will send this to Quantz. You had all better hope that he can repair the flute."

He waved his hand in dismissal and they abandoned their instruments to scurry from the room.

Chapter 20

Ripieno

The palace carriage plodded its way from Potsdam to Berlin. Quantz sat enjoying the last of the day, caring nothing for what was behind nor for any adventures that lay ahead. This was a respite promising an end to their troubles. The new flute would maintain the King's pleasure and his favor. Anna had her new furniture. Their house would grow to hold Stephan and his new apprentice. Heinz kept Anna happy and the boy's interest in everything Stephan taught him had vanquished his ghastly serpent to a forgotten closet. In a very few days, Defutois would follow Heinz to the border and Frederick's pass would bring the man to his home, far from any trouble he may have caused. There would be quietude and the normal rhythms of composition and concerts as predictable as the sun casting warmth into the carriage.

It was with some satisfaction that he thought of them all playing their parts together. This was no time for solo performers, for if anybody stood out, the harmony of what they were accomplishing would be destroyed. If one insisted on performing alone, the stage would become a scaffold from which they would all hang together. The carriage wheels turned in slow circles over the rutted road, but the pace was comforting. There was need for neither the quickness that would reveal their weakness nor lachrymose tears that would betray their fears. No. Courage was a stately thing, plodding as carefully as this horse and accepting whatever shocks would be their lot. He found it funny that in life as in music, an assured execution was necessary.

They entered Potsdam's main street and he listened to the carriage wheels play their gentle staccato over cobble stones.

The blacksmith's anvil added his heavy percussions and Quantz breathed the sweet and pungent aroma blown through the baker's open door. He looked along the line of regimented eaves, each house drawn by a ruler and laughed to think they really did look like Old Fritz' Mushrooms. If the speed and precision of the masons who put up his walls were replicated in all these buildings, Potsdam could double in territory by the time he returned from Bayreuth. He was sure there would be no problems and that Queen Wilhelmina would receive him as an honored guest. He liked her music, but would never confess that she was actually a better musician than her brother. "Judge not, lest ye be judged," he quipped to himself, "or you will be thrown out into the street with the rest of the rubbish."

The carriage soon passed the rows of trees standing guard before each house and Quantz gazed over the fields full of potatoes. Frederick had introduced this new tuber from France. His experts in the Berlin Academy had decided that the potato was a more wholesome food than wheat. His masters of economy had predicted that feeding the peasants on this new vegetable would reduce the cost of agriculture by as much as fifty percent. He wondered on which marvels of artillery Frederick would spend his savings. Every time a new wonder appeared in the kingdom, it seemed to make loud noises, spit fire, and kill. Quantz was grateful to be spared the horrors of the regimental bands. They marched around the quadrangles of parade grounds playing the same tunes as when the army was attacking some faraway hill. The bugles blared, the drums rattled and the flags waved over the maimed and the dead, but the bands played their counterpoint to the screams. If the soldiers were actually musical, they would be bored to death long before any cannon could dispatch then. "If I had to play those infernal ditties, I would welcome the bullet that would put a stop to the racket," he mused. He then remembered that he had said the very same thing after hearing some affected academician play the flute according to the directions in an old, and hopefully, forgotten treatise.

He grumbled to himself about those musicians who could read but not feel. They were ruled by the black dots on the page and loved their enslavement. They were like a traveller who thought he had completed a journey just because he studied a map. It was as useless and as incomprehensible as that idiot he had met in Venice, who thought he could speak German because he bought a dictionary.

He watched the sunlight waft over the green leaves in the fields and assured himself that a "ritornello must be like these plots of blooming vegetation, short and fiery, interspersed at intervals between noisy houses and quiet pastures for contented cows." It was a quick journey from Potsdam to Berlin and not unlike a good concerto "for it was of more advantage if the listeners find a piece too short rather than too long."

The carriage rolled through the tunnel of Berlin's palaces. Courts full of dispute, churches crammed with supplication for forgiveness, halls burgeoning with gay intrigue, they all sang their different songs. Choruses of desire, disappointment, and cowardly resignation. He covered his ears, defending himself from the harsh and discordant clamor of so many people and their crowded lives.

When the carriage thumped onto the bridge over the river, Quantz's eyes followed the golden ribbon of sunset, rippling along its flow. There were few people walking beside the carriage and he caught snatches of laughter and the occasional curse punctuating the thrum of voices. People walked or trudged, tired from their labors, or marched into the evening's revels without regard to the lone gentleman in the carriage. There was safety in their preoccupations and security in his anonymity.

His foot touched the trunk on the carriage's floor. Anna had packed it with her usual care. Each inner wall held a shoe, so he would have three pairs as needed. His best blue coat was clean and stiff from the kettle she had used to clean it. She had a way of boiling spices so the scented steam permeated his clothing. The brush was never sufficient to her demands, so she scoured his coat until the cloth stood proud and breathed of distant lands full of exotic aromas. There were shirts folded over the coats and trousers and placed in the order she considered necessary for wearing day and night. His wig was bagged in old burlap so its powder would not deface his coat. Everything else he wore was simple and suitable for the journey and made him look like a nondescript merchant traveling for his profit.

The music was rolled into a bag and kept in a separate case with his flutes. If it were discovered by some officious border guard, the seal and the signature of the king would be as efficient as the pass in his pocket. He did not think he would need it, for Wilhelmina would have sent a courier to the border post with strict instructions to "offer all aid and assistance to my most welcome guest." The guards would wave them through under the watchful glare and gleaming sabers of Bavarian hussars. When they were safe in Wilhelmina's domains, he would give the pass to Heinz to ease Defutois' passage. On his return journey, the Prussian guards would speed his way home.

The bridge gave way to the open road and he could see the inn at the top of a rise. The coachman snapped his whip, but the horses ignored his commands. They were not going to waste their strength when they could smell fodder and water.

At the summit, Quantz turned to see the sun drop below the western hills and night came as quickly as a final curtain at the opera. Before they stopped, he saw Heinz lounging at the side of the building. The boy looked so bored that no one would notice him, even though he watched every detail. When he saw Quantz, he did not move. There was no rushing to greet the expected traveller. Quantz stepped down from the carriage and Heinz slouched over to ask him, "Help you with your luggage, Sir? Only five pennies." Quantz picked up the little ruse and said, "One trunk." Heinz hefted the trunk with one hand and when he reached for the flutebag, Quantz ordered, "I'll carry that one myself, Boy." Heinz handed Quantz his treasure.

The coachman looked down from his perch and asked, "Shall I wait for you, Sir?" Quantz was quick to tell him, "You have better things to do this evening in Berlin," and handed him a coin. The coachman saw the coin was more than enough to feed and drink and cavort in the best beer caverns of the town. He was eager to get back on the road, now that he could afford so much enjoyment for such a small task as driving one of the courtiers from the palace to the inn. He offered his sincere thanks for Quantz' kindness and turned two very disappointed horses homeward.

Quantz turned to Heinz. "Did you have any trouble finding a coach?" Heinz swung the trunk over his shoulder and told him, "Come see for yourself." Quantz followed Heinz around the inn to the stables. He found an enclosed coach and four horses waiting for him. The coachman was surly and made a great play of being preoccupied with the horses' harness. Quantz returned his gruff manner and demanded, "You know the way to Bayreuth?" The man straightened aggressively. "None better," he almost spat, "for the right price." Quantz gathered all his haughty condescension and said, "Five louis. Six, if you are quick." The coachman's eyes flashed with avarice and he nodded his obvious satisfaction for the fare. "Get ready," Quantz told

Heinz. The boy disappeared around the stable and returned guiding Defutois. "Get in," Quantz ordered and Defutois obeyed with clear apprehension.

Quantz' finger indicated the trunk to the coachman, who scowled at it and proclaimed, "I drive. Your boy loads." Heinz ignored the title of 'boy', picked up the trunk, and slid it through the door onto the floor of the coach. He closed the door and saw a reflection in the window. Quantz was startled by Heinz' exclamation of "Oh Shit" but obeyed his injunction, "Don't turn around."

Quantz looked into the reflections of the window and saw Baron Belfort stagger around the inn with his arms around the shoulders of a muscular boy. He was clearly drunk and in the afterglow of evening, enjoying his companion. They watched Belfort be coaxed to the stable door. Quantz heard some giggling and then the silence of the quiet stable. Without moving, Heinz confessed, "I saw him this afternoon, but he was too busy to see us."

Quantz pushed Heinz into the carriage and commanded the coachman, "Go." He took his seat in front of Heinz and Defutois and drew the curtains over the window. The carriage lurched forward under an insistent whip and he could feel the vehicle turn onto the road. The horses' hooves modulated from a walk to a steady trot and Quantz could feel the inn disappearing behind them.

He thrust his hands into his pockets for the night threatened to be chilly. He looked at Heinz and Defutois and almost whispered, "Everything will be just fine." Defutois remained silent as if not yet convinced. Heinz smiled to the man he had come to admire, the man whose wife had fed and clothed him and gave him the comfort he had never known, and quietly said, "I know."

Quantz' fingers felt the velvet bag he had carefully prepared before leaving home. There were sixty golden circles of louis d'or filling the bag. The new furniture, the dishes, the various things Anna needed as much as she wanted had depleted the money box. Fifty of these last coins he would give to Defutois. They would sustain him on his journey back to France and there might even be enough remaining to help him start his life again. After Bayreuth that would be Defutois' problem. Ten louis would ensure that Heinz would get back to Potsdam without having to walk the whole way. He wondered if Heinz would keep the money, claiming he spent it on the slowest carriage at the greatest price, and hike all the way home. It would be so like the boy to devise some involved tale that no one believed but accepted out of respect for his sheer audacity in telling it. He hoped he would not see the last of Heinz.

The coach crested the hill and the horses quickened into a steady thunder. The coachman took little interest in his passengers. He judged the older man was just another merchant traveling with his servant and his boy. He would keep his eyes on the boy. If this merchant liked the boys, the coachman liked louis even more. He could add to his stock of coins with a promise that he would keep his mouth shut. Blackmail was always a supplement to his journeys, if he could find the evidence.

Quantz rested from the tensions of these many frought weeks. He had tried not to burden Anna for he would not add to her worries. Now was not the time to imagine sudden alarms and painful afflictions. Now was the time to just wait upon fortune under a warm moon.

The Memoir of Charles Defutois

Part the Last

Paris, Lazarette Prison,

July 28, 1794

I will always carry my gratitude for Quantz, as long or as short as I live. That he freed me from my own folly was testament to the man's character and to his decency. But more than this, his gift was to teach me to listen. He had that magic that could tease the beauty from smudges on paper and fill my ears with delight. I will never have his wonders but now I am no longer deaf.

This morning I heard a great tumult beyond the walls rise to the clouds and echo back to earth. Those intrusive cascades rumbled through my cell. Such thunderous joy shot through with the rattle of drummers heralded the end of some great personage.

It sounded very like the day King Louis was executed. What frightening changes come with age. A callow youth, I fainted at the sight of another young man torn asunder. As a man, I shoved my way through the throng to witness a king's head cleft from his body. He stood firm upon the scaffold, bowed to the blade, ignoring the dancers frenzied with vengeful joy. The boys drummed him out of life, but I saw a ravenous monster crawl from that tangled wreck and rise to snatch a thousand crowns. As if one head was fit payment for centuries of past misery and a fee for all the happy futures.

I had hoped that change would bring us relief from the whims of kings and the caprice that dazzles bejeweled heads. But the revolution just eats its own children, a farrowing sow consuming her own young. We fed on fantasies and the heart's grown brutal from the fare.

Two pairs of footsteps hurry down the corridor. I can hear them approaching, one hurried tapping almost running over the other, a plodding bass. I know not what they will bring or if they will take me out of this dreadful place to a swift and silent end. It no longer matters.

Gentle Reader, if you read these words with inky fingers, you will know that I have survived. I will have had a reprieve to bind this story, so you will know of honor on the wind when you most think that only despair remains.

Before I was born, I was not. I live. When I am dead, I will not be. I no longer care. To fret despondent over barren hopes would be waste of breath in the emperor's flute.

Acknowledgments

So many people have contributed to the writing of *The Emperor's Flute* that it is impossible to thank them all.

The first sentence was written while listening to some of the world's greatest flutists play at the Wildacres Flute Retreat. Such talent must be acknowledged as the inspiration for this novel.

Special thanks and my appreciation must be extended to Stephen Preston, Amara Guitry, and Michael Lynn, who all read the manuscript and freely offered their unstinting support and unparalleled knowledge of the Baroque age in general and their expertise in the Baroque flute in particular. Dorothee Oberlinger contributed specific facts and hitherto unknown information, such as Quantz' actual addresses in Potsdam and Berlin. Joy Sears and Ann Overbeck were sensitive and thoughtful readers. To all I owe a deep debt of gratitude.

Anna Thibeault is the source of all inspiration and perspiration in writing *The Emperor's Flute*. Without her love and belief, this would have been impossible.

Thomas Thibeault

Born in Canada, raised in Ireland, lives in the United States, Thomas has retired from a thirty year teaching career which has taken him to Europe, Russia, the Middle East, and the Far East.

Half a century of wide reading, wider traveling, and concentrated thinking have provoked Thomas into writing.

Those travels involved working as a deck hand, soldier, truck driver in Africa, art model in Ireland, train brakeman in Canada, and a tour guide at the pyramids.

Thomas brings a wealth of experience to writing which expresses our primal experiences. He lives in the mountains of Western North Carolina with his wife, Anna, and their ten cats.

photo: Mark Williams Studio

Made in the USA
Lexington, KY
16 November 2019